PRAISE FOR KAREN HESSE'S
OUT OF THE DUST

★ "Hesse's spare prose adroitly traces Billie Jo's journey in and out of darkness. . . . With each meticulously arranged entry she paints a vivid picture of Billie Jo's emotions, ranging from desolation . . . to longing . . . to hope."

— *Publisher's Weekly*, starred review

★ "Hesse uses free-verse poems to advance the plot, allowing the narrator to speak for herself much more eloquently than would be possible in standard prose. The author's astute and careful descriptions of life during the dust storms of the 1930s are grounded in harsh reality, yet are decidedly poetic . . . Hesse's ever growing skill as a writer willing to take chances with her form shines through superbly . . ."

— *School Library Journal*, starred review

★ "The story is bleak, but Hesse's writing transcends the gloom and transforms it into a powerfully compelling tale of a girl with enormous strength, courage and love. The entire novel is written in very readable blank verse, a superb choice for bringing out the exquisite agony and delight to be found in such a difficult period lived by such a vibrant character."

— *Booklist*, starred review

"Hesse presents a hale and determined heroine who confronts unrelenting misery and begins to transcend it. The poem/novel ends with only a trace of hope; there are no pat endings, but a glimpse of beauty wrought from brutal reality."

— *Kirkus Reviews*

". . . The distinctive writing style is . . . remarkably successful . . . filled with memorable images . . . the spare verses showcase the poetry of everyday language; the pauses between line breaks speak eloquently . . . [Billie Jo's] voice, nearly every word informed by longing, provides an immediacy that expressively depicts both a grim historical era and one family's healing."

— *The Horn Book Magazine*

"Hesse evokes the physical realities of the Dust Bowl convincingly, adding details (the sheriff passing on sugar seized from bootleggers to the school, the methodology for finding your way on the road in a dust storm) that bring it to life."

— *BCCB*

"In telling her story, Billie Jo learns about courage, truth and sorrow. . . . The dust storms, the drought and the Depression cannot destroy what grows in the heart. This novel celebrates the tenacity of the human spirit."

— *VOYA*

"With echoes of *Sarah, Plain and Tall*, Hesse's story shows hope growing amid desolation. Billie Jo and her father redefine their relationship and their ideas of what a family can be. . . . *Out of the Dust* seems destined to become her signature work, a literary groundbreaker as stunning as Oklahoma's dust bowl recovery."

— *The Five Owls*

Winner of the Newbery Medal

Winner of the Scott O'Dell Award

An ALA Notable Children's Book

An ALA Best Book for Young Adults

A *School Library Journal* Best Book of the Year

A *Booklist* Editors' Choice

A *Book Links* "Lasting Connection"

A *Publishers Weekly* Best Book of the Year

A New York Public Library
100 Titles for Reading and Sharing selection

APPLE SIGNATURE

Out

of the

Dust

KAREN HESSE

SCHOLASTIC INC.

New York Toronto London Auckland Sydney
Mexico City New Delhi Hong Kong

Cover photograph: courtesy of Library of Congress Prints and Photographs division, Farm Security Administration collection, LC-USF 342-8140A, "Lucille Burroughs, Hale County, Alabama, Summer 1936," by Walker Evans.

ISBN 0-590-37125-8

12 11 10 9 8 7 6 5 4 3 2 1   9/9 0 1 2 3 4/0

Printed in the U.S.A.   40

First Scholastic paperback printing, January 1999

The display face was set in Byron.
The text face was set in Cooper Old Style.
Book design by Elizabeth B. Parisi.

To Brenda Bowen,
who is so much more
than an editor

I extend heartfelt thanks to Eileen Christelow,
Kate, Rachel, and Randy Hesse,
Liza Ketchum, Jeffrey and Bernice Millman,
Maryann Sparks,
and the Oklahoma Historical Society.

Out of the Dust

Winter 1934

Beginning: August 1920

As summer wheat came ripe,
so did I,
born at home, on the kitchen floor.
Ma crouched,
barefoot, bare bottomed
over the swept boards,
because that's where Daddy said it'd be best.

I came too fast for the doctor,
bawling as soon as Daddy wiped his hand around
inside my mouth.
To hear Ma tell it,
I hollered myself red the day I was born.
Red's the color I've stayed ever since.

Daddy named me Billie Jo.
He wanted a boy.
Instead,
he got a long-legged girl
with a wide mouth
and cheekbones like bicycle handles.
He got a redheaded, freckle-faced, narrow-hipped girl
with a fondness for apples
and a hunger for playing fierce piano.

From the earliest I can remember
I've been restless in this
little Panhandle shack we call home,
always getting in Ma's way with my
pointy elbows, my fidgety legs.
By the summer I turned nine Daddy had
given up about having a boy.
He tried making me do.
I look just like him,
I can handle myself most everywhere he puts me,
even on the tractor,
though I don't like that much.

Ma tried having other babies.
It never seemed to go right, except with me.
But this morning
Ma let on as how she's expecting again.
Other than the three of us
there's not much family to speak of.
Daddy, the only boy Kelby left
since Grandpa died
from a cancer
that ate up the most of his skin,
and Aunt Ellis,
almost fourteen years older than Daddy
and living in Lubbock,
a ways south of here,
and a whole world apart

to hear Daddy tell it.
And Ma, with only Great-uncle Floyd,
old as ancient Indian bones,
and mean as a rattler,
rotting away in that room down in Dallas.

I'll be nearly fourteen
just like Aunt Ellis was when Daddy was born
by the time this baby comes.

Wonder if Daddy'll get his boy this time?

January 1934

Rabbit Battles

Mr. Noble and
Mr. Romney have a bet going
as to who can kill the most rabbits.
It all started at the rabbit drive last Monday
over to Sturgis
when Mr. Noble got himself worked up
about the damage done to his crop by jacks.
Mr. Romney swore he'd had more rabbit trouble
than anyone in Cimarron County.
They pledged revenge on the rabbit population;
wagering who could kill more.

They ought to just shut up.
Betting on how many rabbits they can kill.
Honestly!
Grown men clubbing bunnies to death.
Makes me sick to my stomach.
I know rabbits eat what they shouldn't,
especially this time of year when they could hop
halfway to Liberal
and still not find food,
but Miss Freeland says
if we keep
plowing under the stuff they ought to be eating,
what are they supposed to do?

Mr. Noble and
Mr. Romney came home from Sturgis Monday
with twenty rabbits apiece. A tie.
It should've stopped there. But
Mr. Romney wasn't satisfied.
He said,
"Noble cheated.
He brought in rabbits somebody else killed."
And so the contest goes on.

Those men,
they used to be best friends.
Now they can't be civil with each other.
They scowl as they pass on the street.
I'm scowling too,
but scowling won't bring the rabbits back.
They're all skinned and cooked and eaten by now.
At least they didn't end up in
Romney and Noble's cook pots.
They went to families
that needed the meat.

January 1934

Losing Livie

Livie Killian moved away.
I didn't want her to go.
We'd been friends since first grade.

The farewell party was
Thursday night
at the Old Rock Schoolhouse.

Livie
had something to tease each of us about,
like Ray
sleeping through reading class,
and Hillary,
who on her speed-writing test put
an "even ton" of children
instead of an "even ten."

Livie said good-bye to each of us,
separately.
She gave me a picture she'd made of me sitting
in front of a piano,
wearing my straw hat,
an apple halfway to my mouth.

I handed Livie the memory book we'd all
filled with our different slants.

I couldn't get the muscles in my throat relaxed enough
to tell her how much I'd miss her.

Livie
helped clean up her own party,
wiping spilled lemonade,
gathering sandwich crusts,
sweeping cookie crumbs from the floor,
while the rest of us went home
to study for semester reviews.

Now Livie's gone west,
out of the dust,
on her way to California,
where the wind takes a rest sometimes.
And I'm wondering what kind of friend I am,
wanting my feet on that road to another place,
instead of Livie's.

January 1934

Me and Mad Dog

Arley Wanderdale,
who teaches music once a week at our school,
though Ma says he's no teacher at all,
just a local song plugger,
Arley Wanderdale asked
if I'd like to play a piano solo
at the Palace Theatre on Wednesday night.

I grinned,
pleased to be asked, and said,
"That'd be all right."

I didn't know if Ma would let me.
She's an old mule on the subject of my schooling.
She says,
"You stay home on weeknights, Billie Jo."
And mostly that's what I do.

But Arley Wanderdale said,
"The management asked me to
bring them talent, Billie Jo,
and I thought of you."

Even before Mad Dog Craddock? I wondered.

"You and Mad Dog," Arley Wanderdale said.

Darn that blue-eyed boy
with his fine face and his
smooth voice,
twice as good
as a plowboy has any right to be.
I suspected Mad Dog had come first
to Arley Wanderdale's mind,
but I didn't get too riled.
Not so riled I couldn't say yes.

January 1934

Permission to Play

Sometimes,
when Ma is busy in the kitchen,
or scrubbing,
or doing wash,
I can ask her something in such a way
I annoy her just enough to get an answer,
but not so much I get a no.

That's a way I've found of gaining what I want,
by catching Ma off guard,
especially when I'm after permission to play piano.
Right out asking her is no good.
She always gets testy about me playing,
even though she's the one who truly taught me.

Anyway, this time I caught her in the
slow stirring of biscuits,
her mind on other things,
maybe the baby growing inside her, I don't know,
but anyhow,
she was distracted enough,
I was determined enough,
this time I got just what I wanted.
Permission to play at the Palace.

January 1934

On Stage

When I point my fingers at the keys,
                     the music
springs straight out of me.
                     Right hand
playing notes sharp as
                     tongues,
telling stories while the
                     smooth
buttery rhythms back me up
                     on the left.

Folks sway in the
                     Palace aisles
grinning and stomping and
                     out of breath,
and the rest, eyes shining,
                     fingers snapping,
feet tapping. It's the best
                     I've ever felt,
playing hot piano,
                     sizzling with
Mad Dog,
                     swinging with the Black Mesa Boys,
or on my own,
                     crazy,

pestering the keys.
                    That is
heaven.
                    How supremely
heaven
                    playing piano
can be.

January 1934

Birthday for F.D.R.

I played so well
on Wednesday night,
Arley put his arm across my shoulder
and asked me to come and
perform at the President's birthday ball.
Ma can't say no to this one.
It's for President Roosevelt.
Not that Mr. Roosevelt will actually be there,
but the money collected at the ball,
along with balls all over the country,
will go,
in the President's name,
to the Warm Springs Foundation,
where Mr. Roosevelt stayed once when he was sick.

Someday,
I plan to play for President Franklin Delano Roosevelt
himself.
Maybe I'll go all the way to the White House in
Washington, D.C.
In the meantime,
it's pretty nice
Arley asking me to play twice,
for Joyce City.

January 1934

Not Too Much To Ask

We haven't had a good crop in three years,
not since the bounty of '31,
and we're all whittled down to the bone these days,
even Ma, with her new round belly,
but still
when the committee came asking,
Ma donated:
three jars of apple sauce
and
some cured pork,
and a
feed-sack nightie she'd sewn for our coming baby.

February 1934

Mr. Hardly's Money Handling

It was Daddy's birthday
and Ma decided to bake him a cake.
There wasn't
money enough for anything like a real present.
Ma sent me to fetch the extras
with fifty cents she'd been hiding away.
"Don't go to Joyce City, Billie," she said.
"You can get what we need down Hardly's store."

I slipped the coins into my sweater pocket, the pocket
without the hole,
thinking about how many sheets of new music
fifty cents would buy.

Mr. Hardly glared
when the Wonder Bread door
banged shut behind me.
He squinted as I creaked across the wooden floor.
Mr. Hardly was in the habit
of charging too much for his stale food,
and he made bad change when he thought
he could get away with it.
I squinted back at him as I gave him Ma's order.

Mr. Hardly's
been worse than normal

since his attic filled with dust
and collapsed under the weight.
He hired folks for the repairs,
and argued over every nail and every
little minute.
The whole place took
shoveling for days before he could
open again and
some stock was so bad it
had to be thrown away.

The stove clanked in the corner
as Mr. Hardly filled Ma's order.
I could smell apples,
ground coffee, and peppermint.
I sorted through the patterns on the feed bags,
sneezed dust,
blew my nose.

When Mr. Hardly finished sacking my things,
I paid the bill,
and tucking the list in my pocket along with the
change,
hurried home,
so Ma could bake the cake before Daddy came in.

But after Ma emptied the sack,
setting each packet out on the

oilcloth, she counted her change
and I remembered with a sinking feeling
that I hadn't kept an eye on
Mr. Hardly's money handling,
and Mr. Hardly had cheated again.
Only this time he'd cheated himself, giving us
four cents extra.

So while Ma mixed a cake,
I walked back to Mr. Hardly's store,
back through the dust,
back through the Wonder Bread door,
and thinking about the secondhand music
in a moldy box at the shop in Joyce City,
music I could have for two cents a sheet,
I placed Mr. Hardly's overpayment on the counter
and turned to head back home.

Mr. Hardly cleared his throat and
I wondered for a moment
if he'd call me back to offer a piece of peppermint
or pick me out an apple from the crate,
but he didn't,
and that's okay.
Ma would have thrown a fit
if I'd taken a gift from him.

February 1934

Fifty Miles South of Home

In Amarillo,
wind
blew plate-glass windows in,
tore electric signs down,
ripped wheat
straight out of the ground.

February 1934

Rules of Dining

Ma has rules for setting the table.
I place plates upside down,
glasses bottom side up,
napkins folded over forks, knives, and spoons.

When dinner is ready,
we sit down together
and Ma says,
"Now."

We shake out our napkins,
spread them on our laps,
and flip over our glasses and plates,
exposing neat circles,
round comments
on what life would be without dust.

Daddy says,
"The potatoes are peppered plenty tonight, Polly,"
and
"Chocolate milk for dinner, aren't we in clover!"
when really all our pepper and chocolate,
it's nothing but dust.

I heard word from Livie Killian.
The Killians can't find work,

can't get food.
Livie's brother, Reuben, fifteen last summer,
took off, thinking to make it on his own.
I hope he's okay.

With a baby growing inside Ma,
it scares me thinking, Where would we be without
somewhere to live?
Without some work to do?
Without something to eat?
At least we've got milk. Even if we have to chew it.

February 1934

Breaking Drought

After seventy days
of wind and sun,
of wind and clouds,
of wind and sand,
after seventy days,
of wind and dust,
a little
rain
came.

February 1934

Dazzled

In the kitchen she is my ma,
in the barn and the fields she is my daddy's wife,
but in the parlor Ma is something different.
She isn't much to look at,
so long and skinny,
her teeth poor,
her dark hair always needing a wash, but
from the time I was four,
I remember being dazzled by her
whenever she played the piano.

Daddy bought it, an old Cramer,
his wedding gift to her.
She came to this house and found gaps in the walls,
a rusty bed, no running water,
and that piano,
gleaming in the corner.

Daddy gets soft eyes, standing behind her while she
plays.
I want someone to look that way at me.

On my fifth birthday,
Ma sat me down beside her
and started me to reading music,
started me to playing.

I'm not half so good as Ma.
She can pull Daddy into the parlor
even after the last milking, when he's so beat
he barely knows his own name
and all he wants
is a mattress under his bones.
You've got to be something
to get his notice that time of day,
but Ma can.
I'm not half so good with my crazy playing
as she is with her fine tunes and her
fancy fingerwork.
But I'm good enough for Arley, I guess.

March 1934

Debts

Daddy is thinking
of taking a loan from Mr. Roosevelt and his men,
to get some new wheat planted
where the winter crop has spindled out and died.
Mr. Roosevelt promises
Daddy won't have to pay a dime
till the crop comes in.

Daddy says,
"I can turn the fields over,
start again.
It's sure to rain soon.
Wheat's sure to grow."

Ma says, "What if it doesn't?"

Daddy takes off his hat,
roughs up his hair,
puts the hat back on.
"Course it'll rain," he says.

Ma says, "Bay,
it hasn't rained enough to grow wheat in
three years."

Daddy looks like a fight brewing.

He takes that red face of his out to the barn,
to keep from feuding with my pregnant ma.

I ask Ma
how,
after all this time,
Daddy still believes in rain.

"Well, it rains enough," Ma says,
"now and again,
to keep a person hoping.
But even if it didn't
your daddy would have to believe.
It's coming on spring,
and he's a farmer."

March 1934

Foul as Maggoty Stew

Arley Wanderdale said
the rehearsals for *Sunny of Sunnyside*
shouldn't take me out of school
more than twice next week.

When I told Ma she got angry about
my missing school to play piano for some show.

Me and Daddy,
we're trying our best to please Ma,
for fear of what it might do to the baby if we don't.
I don't know why she's
so against my playing.
She says that school is important,
but I do all right in school.
I know she doesn't like the kind
of music I play,
but sometimes I think she's
just plain jealous
when I'm at the piano
and she's not.
And maybe she's a little afraid
of me going somewhere with the music
she can't follow.
Or of the music taking me
so far away one day

I'll never come home.
Whatever the reason, she said I couldn't do it.
Arley had to get somebody to take my place.

I do as she says. I go to school,
and in the afternoons I come home,
run through my chores,
do my reading and my math work at the
kitchen table
and all the while I glare at Ma's back with a scowl
foul as maggoty stew.

March 1934

State Tests

When I got home I told Ma
our school scored higher than the
whole state on achievement tests and
I scored top of eighth grade.

Ma nodded.
"I knew you could."

That's all she said.

She was proud,
I could tell.
But she didn't
coo like Mad Dog's ma. Or
go on
like Mrs. Killian used to do.
Daddy says,
"That's not your ma's way."
But I wish it was.
I wish she'd give me a little more to hold on to than
"I knew you could."
Instead she makes me feel like she's just
taking me in like I was
so much flannel dry on the line.

March 1934

Fields of Flashing Light

I heard the wind rise,
and stumbled from my bed,
down the stairs,
out the front door,
into the yard.
The night sky kept flashing,
lightning danced down on its spindly legs.

I sensed it before I knew it was coming.
I heard it,
smelled it,
tasted it.
Dust.

While Ma and Daddy slept,
the dust came,
tearing up fields where the winter wheat,
set for harvest in June,
stood helpless.
I watched the plants,
surviving after so much drought and so much wind,
I watched them fry,
or
flatten,
or blow away,
like bits of cast-off rags.

It wasn't until the dust turned toward the house,
like a fired locomotive,
and I fled,
barefoot and breathless, back inside,
it wasn't until the dust
hissed against the windows,
until it ratcheted the roof,
that Daddy woke.

He ran into the storm,
his overalls half-hooked over his union suit.
"Daddy!" I called. "You can't stop dust."

Ma told me to
cover the beds,
push the scatter rugs against the doors,
dampen the rags around the windows.
Wiping dust out of everything,
she made coffee and biscuits,
waiting for Daddy to come in.

Sometime after four,
rubbing low on her back,
Ma sank down into a chair at the kitchen table
and covered her face.
Daddy didn't come back for hours,
not
until the temperature dropped so low,
it brought snow.

Ma and I sighed, grateful,
staring out at the dirty flakes,
but our relief didn't last.
The wind snatched that snow right off the fields,
leaving behind a sea of dust,
waves and
waves and
waves of
dust,
rippling across our yard.

Daddy came in,
he sat across from Ma and blew his nose.
Mud streamed out.
He coughed and spit out
mud.
If he had cried,
his tears would have been mud too,
but he didn't cry.
And neither did Ma.

March 1934

Spring 1934 _____

Tested by Dust

While we sat
taking our six-weeks test,
the wind rose
and the sand blew
right through the cracks in the schoolhouse wall,
right through the gaps around the window glass,
and by the time the tests were done,
each and every one of us
was coughing pretty good and we all
needed a bath.

I hope we get bonus points
for testing in a dust storm.

April 1934

Banks

Ma says,
everything we lost
when the banks closed
'cause they didn't have enough cash to go around,
all the money that's ours
is coming back to us in full.

Good.

Now we have money for a doctor
when the baby comes.

April 1934

Beat Wheat

County Agent Dewey
had some pretty bad news.
One quarter of the wheat is lost:
blown away or withered up.
What remains is little more than
a wisp of what it should be.
And every day we have no rain,
more wheat dies.

County Agent Dewey says, "Soon
there won't be enough wheat
for seed to plant next fall."

The piano is some comfort in all this.
I go to it and I forget the dust for hours,
testing my long fingers on wild rhythms,
but Ma slams around in the kitchen when I play
and after a while she sends me to the store.
Joe De La Flor doesn't see me pass him by;
he rides his fences, dazed by dust.
I wince at the sight of his rib-thin cattle.
But he's not even seeing them.
I look at Joe and know our future is drying up
and blowing away with the dust.

April 1934

Give Up on Wheat

Ma says,
"Try putting in a pond, Bayard.
We can fill it off the windmill.
We've got a good well."

Daddy grumbles, "The water'll seep
back into the ground
as fast as I can pump it, Pol.
We'll dry up our well
and then we'll have nothing."

"Plant some other things, then," Ma says.
"Try cotton,
sorghum. If we plant the fields in different crops,
maybe some will do better,
better than wheat."

Daddy says,
"No.
It has to be wheat.
I've grown it before.
I'll grow it again."

But Ma says, "Can't you see
what's happening, Bayard?
The wheat's not meant to be here."

And Daddy says,
"What about those apple trees of yours, Pol?
You think they are?
Nothing needs more to drink than those two.
But you wouldn't hear of leveling your apples,
would you?"

Ma is bittering. I can see it in her mouth.
"A pond would work," she says,
sounding crusty and stubborn.

And Daddy says, "Look it, Pol, who's the farmer?
You or me?"

Ma says,
"Who pays the bills?"

"No one right now," Daddy says.

Ma starts to quaking but she won't let Daddy see.
Instead, she goes out to the chickens
and
her anger,
simmering over like a pot in an empty kitchen,
boils itself down doing chores.

April 1934

What I Don't Know

My teacher, Miss Freeland,
is singing
at the Shrine
along with famous
opera stars
from all around the country
in a play called
Madame Butterfly.

I've never heard of that play.

"Most everyone's heard of *Madame Butterfly*,"
Mad Dog says.

How does that
singing plowboy know something I don't?
And how much more is out there
most everyone else has heard of
except me?

April 1934

Apple Blossoms

Ma
has been nursing these two trees
for as long as I can remember.
In spite of the dust,
in spite of the drought,
because of Ma's stubborn care,
these trees are
thick with blossoms,
delicate and
pinky-white.

My eyes can't get enough of the sight of them.
I stand under the trees
and let the petals
fall into my hair,
a blizzard
of sweet-smelling flowers,
dropped from the boughs of the two
placed there
in the front yard by Ma
before I was born,
that she and they might bring forth fruit
into our home,
together.

May 1934

World War

Daddy was just seventeen
when he fought in the
Great War off in France.

There's not much he's willing to
say about those days, except about the poppies.
He remembers the poppies,
red on the graves of the dead.

Daddy says
that war tore France up
worse than a tornado,
worse than a dust storm,
but no matter,
the wild poppies bloomed in the trail of the fighting,
brightening the French countryside.

I wish I could see poppies
growing out of this dust.

May 1934

Apples

Ma's apple blossoms
have turned to hard green balls.

To eat them now,
so tart,
would turn my mouth inside out,
would make my stomach groan.

But in just a couple months,
after the baby is born,
those apples will be ready
and we'll make pies
and sauce
and pudding
and dumplings
and cake
and cobbler
and have just plain apples to take to school
and slice with my pocket knife
and eat one juicy piece at a time
until my mouth is clean
and fresh
and my breath is nothing but apple.

June 1934

Dust and Rain

On Sunday,
winds came,
bringing a red dust
like prairie fire,
hot and peppery,
searing the inside of my nose,
the whites of my eyes.
Roaring dust,
turning the day from sunlight to midnight.

And as the dust left,
rain came.
Rain that was no blessing.
It came too hard,
too fast,
and washed the soil away,
washed the wheat away with it.
Now
little remains of Daddy's hard work.
And the only choice he has
is to give up or
start all over again.

At the Strong ranch
they didn't get a single drop.
So who fared better?

Ma looks out the window at her apple trees.
Hard green balls have dropped to the ground.
But there are enough left;
enough
for a small harvest,
if we lose no more.

June 1934

Harvest

The combines have started moving across the fields,
bringing in wheat,
whatever has managed to grow.

Mr. Tuttle delivered the first load to town
selling it for seventy-three cents a bushel.
Not bad.

Mr. Chaffin, Mr. Haverstick, and Mr. French,
they've delivered their harvest too,
dropping it at the Joyce City grain elevator.

Daddy asked Mr. Haverstick how things looked
and Mr. Haverstick said he figures
he took eight bushels off a twenty-bushel acre.

If Daddy gets five bushels to his acre
it'll be a miracle.

June 1934

On the Road with Arley

Here's the way I figure it.
My place in the world is at the piano.
I'm earning a little money playing,
thanks to Arley Wanderdale.
He and his Black Mesa Boys have connections in
Keyes and Goodwell and Texhoma.
And every little crowd
is grateful to hear a rag or two played
on the piano
by a long-legged, red-haired girl,
even when the piano has a few keys soured by dust.

At first Ma crossed her arms
against her chest
and stared me down,
hard-jawed and sharp, and said I couldn't go.
But the money helped convince her,
and the compliment from Arley and his wife, Vera,
that they'd surely bring my ma along to play too,
if she wasn't so far gone with a baby coming.
Ma said
okay,
but only for the summer,
and only if she didn't hear me gripe how I was tired,
or see me dragging my back end around,
or have to call me twice upon a morning,

or find my farm chores falling down,
and only if Arley's wife, Vera, kept an eye on me.

Arley says my piano playing is good.
I play a set of songs with the word *baby* in the title,
like "My Baby Just Cares for Me"
and "Walking My Baby Back Home."
I picked those songs on purpose for Ma,
and the folks that come to hear Arley's band,
they like them fine.

Arley pays in dimes.
Ma's putting my earnings away I don't know where,
saving it to send me to school in a few years.
The money doesn't matter much to me.
I'd play for nothing.
When I'm with Arley's boys we forget the dust.
We are flying down the road in Arley's car,
singing,
laying our voices on top of the
beat Miller Rice plays on the back of Arley's seat,
and sometimes, Vera, up front, chirps crazy notes with
no words
and the sounds she makes seem just about amazing.

It's being part of all that,
being part of Arley's crowd I like so much,
being on the road,

being somewhere new and interesting.
We have a fine time.

And they let me play piano, too.

June 1934

Summer 1934

Hope in a Drizzle

Quarter inch of rain
is nothing to complain about.
It'll help the plants above ground,
and start the new seeds growing.

That quarter inch of rain did wonders for Ma, too,
who is ripe as a melon these days.
She has nothing to say to anyone anymore,
except how she aches for rain,
at breakfast,
at dinner,
all day,
all night,
she aches for rain.

Today, she stood out in the drizzle
hidden from the road,
and from Daddy,
and she thought from me,
but I could see her from the barn,
she was bare as a pear,
raindrops
sliding down her skin,
leaving traces of mud on her face and her long back,
trickling dark and light paths,

slow tracks of wet dust down the bulge of her belly.
My dazzling ma, round and ripe and striped
like a melon.

July 1934

Dionne Quintuplets

While the dust blew
down our road,
against our house,
across our fields,
up in Canada
a lady named Elzire Dionne
gave birth to five baby girls
all at once.

I looked at Ma,
so pregnant with one baby.
"Can you imagine five?" I said.
Ma lowered herself into a chair.
Tears dropping on her tight stretched belly,
she wept
just to think of it.

July 1934

Wild Boy of the Road

A boy came by the house today,
he asked for food.
He couldn't pay anything, but Ma set him down
and gave him biscuits
and milk.
He offered to work for his meal,
Ma sent him out to see Daddy.
The boy and Daddy came back late in the afternoon.
The boy walked two steps behind,
in Daddy's dust.
He wasn't more than sixteen.
Thin as a fence rail.
I wondered what
Livie Killian's brother looked like now.
I wondered about Livie herself.
Daddy asked if the boy wanted a bath,
a haircut,
a change of clothes before he moved on.
The boy nodded.
I never heard him say more than "Yes, sir" or
"No, sir" or
"Much obliged."

We watched him walk away
down the road,
in a pair of Daddy's mended overalls,

his legs like willow limbs,
his arms like reeds.
Ma rested her hands on her heavy stomach,
Daddy rested his chin on the top of my head.
"His mother is worrying about him," Ma said.
"His mother is wishing her boy would come home."

Lots of mothers wishing that these days,
while their sons walk to California,
where rain comes,
and the color green doesn't seem like such a miracle,
and hope rises daily, like sap in a stem.
And I think, some day I'm going to walk there too,
through New Mexico and Arizona and Nevada.
Some day I'll leave behind the wind, and the dust
and walk my way West
and make myself to home in that distant place
of green vines and promise.

July 1934

The Accident

I got
burned
bad.

Daddy
put a pail of kerosene
next to the stove
and Ma,
fixing breakfast,
thinking the pail was
filled with water,
lifted it,
to make Daddy's coffee,
poured it,
but instead of making coffee,
Ma made a rope of fire.
It rose up from the stove
to the pail
and the kerosene burst
into flames.

Ma ran across the kitchen,
out the porch door,
screaming for Daddy.
I tore after her,
then,

thinking of the burning pail
left behind in the bone-dry kitchen,
I flew back and grabbed it,
throwing it out the door.

I didn't know.
I didn't know Ma was coming back.

The flaming oil
splashed
onto her apron,
and Ma,
suddenly Ma,
was a column of fire.
I pushed her to the ground,
desperate to save her,
desperate to save the baby, I
tried,
beating out the flames with my hands.
I did the best I could.
But it was no good.
Ma
got
burned
bad.

July 1934

Burns

At first I felt no pain,
only heat.

I thought I might be swallowed by the heat,
like the witch in "Hansel and Gretel,"
and nothing would be left of me.

Someone brought Doc Rice.
He tended Ma first,
then came to me.
The doctor cut away the skin on my hands, it hung in
crested strips.
He cut my skin away with scissors,
then poked my hands with pins to see what I could
feel.
He bathed my burns in antiseptic.

Only then the pain came.

July 1934

Nightmare

I am awake now,
still shaking from my dream:

I was coming home
through a howling dust storm,
my lowered face was scrubbed raw by dirt and wind.
Grit scratched my eyes,
it crunched between my teeth.
Sand chafed inside my clothes,
against my skin.
Dust crept inside my ears, up my nose,
down my throat.
I shuddered, nasty with dust.

In the house,
dust blew through the cracks in the walls,
it covered the floorboards and
heaped against the doors.
It floated in the air, everywhere.
I didn't care about anyone, anything, only the piano. I
searched for it,
found it under a mound of dust.
I was angry at Ma for letting in the dust.
I cleaned off the keys
but when I played,
a tortured sound came from the piano,

like someone shrieking.
I hit the keys with my fist, and the piano broke into
a hundred pieces.

Daddy called to me. He asked me to bring water,
Ma was thirsty.
I brought up a pail of fire and Ma drank it. She had
given birth to a baby of flames. The baby
burned at her side.

I ran away. To the Eatons' farm.
The house had been tractored out,
tipped off its foundation.
No one could live there.
Everywhere I looked were dunes of rippled dust.
The wind roared like fire.
The door to the house hung open and there was
dust inside
several feet deep.
And there was a piano.

The bench was gone, right through the floor.
The piano leaned toward me.
I stood and played.
The relief I felt to hear the sound of music after the
sound
of the piano at home. . . .

I dragged the Eatons' piano through the dust
to our house,
but when I got it there I couldn't play. I had swollen
lumps for hands,
they dripped a sickly pus,
they swung stupidly from my wrists,
they stung with pain.

When I woke up, the part
about my hands
was real.

July 1934

A Tent of Pain

Daddy
has made a tent out of the sheet over Ma
so nothing will touch her skin,
what skin she has left.
I can't look at her,
I can't recognize her.
She smells like scorched meat.
Her body groaning there,
it looks nothing like my ma.
It doesn't even have a face.

Daddy brings her water,
and drips it inside the slit of her mouth
by squeezing a cloth.
She can't open her eyes,
she cries out
when the baby moves inside her,
otherwise she moans,
day and night.
I wish the dust would plug my ears
so I couldn't hear her.

July 1934

Drinking

Daddy found the money
Ma kept squirreled in the kitchen under the
threshold.

It wasn't very much.
But it was enough for him to get good and drunk.

He went out last night.
While Ma moaned and begged for water.
He drank up the emergency money
until it was gone.

I tried to help her.
I couldn't aim the dripping cloth into her mouth.
I couldn't squeeze.
It hurt the blisters on my hands to try.
I only made it worse for Ma. She cried
for the pain of the water running into her sores,
she cried for the water that
would not soothe her throat
and quench her thirst,
and the whole time
my father was in Guymon,
drinking.

July 1934

Devoured

Doc sent me outside to get water.
The day was so hot,
the house was so hot.
As I came out the door,
I saw the cloud descending.
It whirred like a thousand engines.
It shifted shape as it came
settling first over Daddy's wheat.
Grasshoppers,
eating tassles, leaves, stalks.
Then coming closer to the house,
eating Ma's garden, the fence posts,
the laundry on the line, and then,
the grasshoppers came right over me,
descending on Ma's apple trees.
I climbed into the trees,
opening scabs on my tender hands,
grasshoppers clinging to me.
I tried beating them away.
But the grasshoppers ate every leaf,
they ate every piece of fruit.
Nothing left but a couple apple cores,
hanging from Ma's trees.
I couldn't tell her,
couldn't bring myself to say

her apples were gone.
I never had a chance.

Ma died that day
giving birth to my brother.

August 1934

Blame

My father's sister came to fetch my brother,
even as Ma's body cooled.
She came to bring my brother back to Lubbock
to raise as her own,
but my brother died before Aunt Ellis got here.
She wouldn't even hold his little body.
She barely noticed me.
As soon as she found my brother dead,
she
had a talk with my father.
Then she turned around
and headed back to Lubbock.

The neighbor women came.
They wrapped my baby brother in a blanket
and placed him in Ma's bandaged arms.
We buried them together
on the rise Ma loved,
the one she gazed at from the kitchen window,
the one that looks out over the
dried-up Beaver River.

Reverend Bingham led the service.
He talked about Ma,
but what he said made no sense
and I could tell

he didn't truly know her,
he'd never even heard her play piano.
He asked my father
to name my baby brother.
My father, hunched over, said nothing.
I spoke up in my father's silence.
I told the reverend
my brother's name was Franklin.
Like our President.

The women talked as they
scrubbed death from our house.
I
stayed in my room
silent on the iron bed,
listening to their voices.

"Billie Jo threw the pail,"
they said. "An accident,"
they said.
Under their words a finger pointed.

They didn't talk
about my father leaving kerosene by the stove.
They didn't say a word about my father
drinking himself
into a stupor
while Ma writhed, begging for water.

They only said,
Billie Jo threw the pail of kerosene.

August 1934

Birthday

I walk to town.
I don't look back over my shoulder
at the single grave
holding Ma and my little brother.
I am trying not to look back at anything.

Dust rises with each step,
there's a greasy smell to the air.
On either side of the road are
the carcasses of jackrabbits, small birds, field mice,
stretching out into the distance.

My father stares out across his land,
empty but for a few withered stalks
like the tufts on an old man's head.
I don't know if he thinks more of Ma,
or the wheat that used to grow here.

There is barely a blade of grass
swaying in the stinging wind,
there are only these
lumps of flesh
that once were hands long enough to span octaves,
swinging at my sides.

I come up quiet
and sit behind Arley Wanderdale's house,
where no one can see me, and lean my head back,
and close my eyes,
and listen to Arley play.

August 1934

Roots

President Roosevelt tells us to
plant trees. Trees will
break the wind. He says,
trees
will end the drought,
the animals can take shelter there,
children can take shelter.
Trees have roots, he says.
They hold on to the land.

That's good advice, but
I'm not sure he understands the problem.

Trees have never been at home here.
They're just not meant to be here.
Maybe none of us are meant to be here,
only the prairie grass
and the hawks.

My father will stay, no matter what,
he's stubborn as sod.
He and the land have a hold on each other.
But what about me?

August 1934

The Empty Spaces

I don't know my father anymore.
He sits across from me,
he looks like my father,
he chews his food like my father,
he brushes his dusty hair back
like my father,
but he is a stranger.

I am awkward with him,
and irritated,
and I want to be alone
but I am terrified of being alone.

We are both changing,
we are shifting to fill in the empty spaces left by Ma.
I keep my raw and stinging hands
behind my back when he comes near
because he
stares
when he sees them.

September 1934

The Hole

The heat from the cookstove hurts my burns,
and the salt,
the water, and the dust hurt too.
I spend all my time in pain,
and
my father spends his time out the side of the house,
digging a hole,
forty feet by sixty feet,
six feet deep.

I think he is digging the pond,
to feed off the windmill,
the one Ma wanted,
but he doesn't say. He just digs.

He sends me to the train yard to gather boards,
boards that once were box cars
but now are junk.
I bring them back, careful of the scabs and the
raw sores on my bare hands.
I don't know what he needs boards for.
He doesn't tell me.

When he's not in the hole, digging,
he works on the windmill,

replacing the parts
that kept it from turning.

People stop by and watch. They think my father is
crazy
digging such a big hole.
I think he's crazy too.
The water will seep back into the earth.
It'll never stay put in any old pond.
But my father has thought through all that
and he's digging anyway.

I think to talk to Ma about it,
and then I remember.

I can almost forgive him the taking of Ma's money,
I can almost forgive him his night in Guymon,
getting drunk.
But as long as I live,
no matter how big a hole he digs,
I can't forgive him that pail of kerosene
left by the side of the stove.

September 1934

Kilauea

A volcano erupted in Hawaii.
Kilauea.
It threw huge
chunks
into the air,
the ground shook,
and smoke
choked everything in its path.

. . . sounds a little
like a dust storm.

September 1934

Boxes

In my closet are two boxes,
the gatherings of my life,
papers,
school drawings,
a broken hairpin,
a dress from my baby days,
my first lock of hair,
a tiny basket woven from prairie grass,
a doll with a china head,
a pink ball,
three dozen marbles,
a fan from Baxter's Funeral Home,
my baby teeth in a glass jar,
a torn map of the world,
two candy wrappers,
a thousand things I haven't looked at
in years.
I kept promising to go through the boxes
with Ma
and get rid of what I didn't need,
but I never got to it
and now my hands hurt.
And I haven't got the heart.

September 1934

Night Bloomer

Mrs. Brown's
cereus plant bloomed on Saturday night.
She sent word
after promising I could come see it.
I rubbed my gritty eyes with swollen hands.
My stomach grizzled as I
made my way through the dark
to her house.
Ma wouldn't have let me go at all.
My father just stood in the doorway and
watched me leave.

It was almost three in the morning when I got there.
A small crowd stood around.
Mrs. Brown said,
"The blossom opened at midnight,
big as a dinner plate.
It took only moments to unfold."

How can such a flower
find a way to bloom in this drought,
in this wind.

It blossomed at night,
when the sun couldn't scorch it,
when the wind was quiet,

when there might have been a sip of dew
to freshen it.

I couldn't watch at dawn,
when the flower,
touched by the first finger of morning light,
wilted and died.
I couldn't watch
as the tender petals burned up in the sun.

September 1934

The Path of Our Sorrow

Miss Freeland said,
"During the Great War we fed the world.
We couldn't grow enough wheat
to fill all the bellies.
The price the world paid for our wheat
was so high
it swelled our wallets
and our heads,
and we bought bigger tractors,
more acres,
until we had mortgages
and rent
and bills
beyond reason,
but we all felt so useful, we didn't notice.
Then the war ended and before long,
Europe didn't need our wheat anymore,
they could grow their own.
But we needed Europe's money
to pay our mortgage,
our rent,
our bills.
We squeezed more cattle,
more sheep,
onto less land,
and they grazed down the stubble

till they reached root.
And the price of wheat kept dropping
so we had to grow more bushels
to make the same amount of money we made before,
to pay for all that equipment, all that land,
and the more sod we plowed up,
the drier things got,
because the water that used to collect there
under the grass,
biding its time,
keeping things alive through the dry spells
wasn't there anymore.
Without the sod the water vanished,
the soil turned to dust.
Until the wind took it,
lifting it up and carrying it away.
Such a sorrow doesn't come suddenly,
there are a thousand steps to take
before you get there."
But now,
sorrow climbs up our front steps,
big as Texas, and we didn't even see it coming,
even though it'd been making its way straight for us
all along.

September 1934

Autumn 1934

Hired Work

My father hired on
at Wireless Power on Tuesday,
excavating for towers.

He said,
"I'm good at digging,"
and everyone who knows about our hole
knows he's telling the truth.

He might as well earn a couple dollars.
It doesn't look good for the winter crop.
Earning some cash will make him feel better.
I don't think he'll drink it up.
He hasn't done that since Ma

It's hard to believe I once brought money in too,
even if it was just a dime now and then,
for playing piano.
Now I can't hardly stay in the same room with one.
Especially Ma's.

October 1934

Almost Rain

It almost rained Saturday.
The clouds hung low over the farm.
The air felt thick.
It smelled like rain.

In town,
the sidewalks
got damp.
That was all.

November 1934

Those Hands

The Wildcats started practice this week.
Coach Albright used to say I could play for the team.
"You've got what it takes, Billie Jo.
Look at the size of those hands," he'd say. "Look at
how tall."
I'd tell him, "Just because I'm tall doesn't mean I can
play basketball,
or even that I want to."
But he'd say I should play anyway.

Coach Albright didn't say anything to me about
basketball this year.
I haven't gotten any shorter.
It's because of my hands.

My father used to say, why not put those hands to
good use?
He doesn't say anything about "those hands"
anymore.
Only Arley Wanderdale talks about them,
and how they could play piano again,
if I would only try.

November 1934

Real Snow

The dust stopped,
and it
snowed.
Real snow.
Dreamy Christmas snow,
gentle,
nothing blowing,
such calm,
like after a fever,
wet,
clinging to the earth,
melting into the dirt,
snow.

Oh, the grass, and the wheat
and the cattle,
and the rabbits,
and my father will be happy.

November 1934

Dance Revue

Vera Wanderdale
is putting on a dance revue at the Palace
and Arley asked
if I'd play a number with the Black Mesa Boys.
It's hard, coming on to Christmas,
just me and my father,
with no Ma and no little brother.
I don't really feel like doing anything.
Still, I told Arley I would try,
just because it looked like it meant a lot to him.
He said he'd be dancing then,
so he needed a piano player,
and Mad Dog would be singing,
and he knew how I'd just love to be
connected with anything Mad Dog's doing.

The costumes Vera ordered
come all the way from the city, she said.
Special,
the latest cuts.
I wish I could go with her
to pick them up.

During rehearsals,
Mad Dog comes off the stage after his numbers
and stands by the piano.

He doesn't look at me like
I'm a poor motherless thing.
He doesn't stare at my deformed hands.
He looks at me like I am
someone he knows,
someone named Billie Jo Kelby.
I'm grateful for that,
especially considering how bad I'm playing.

December 1934

Mad Dog's Tale

Mad Dog is surrounded by girls.
They ask him how he got his name.
He says, "It's not because I'm wild,
or a crazy, untamed boy,
but because fourteen years ago when I was two
I would bite anything I could catch hold of: my ma,
my brother, Doc Rice, even Reverend Bingham.
So my father named me Mad Dog.
And it stuck."

When I go home
I ask my father if he knows Mad Dog's
real name.
He looks at me like I'm talking in another language.

Ma could have told me.

December 1934

Art Exhibit

We had an art exhibit last week
in the basement of the courthouse,
to benefit the library.
Price of admission was one book
or ten cents.
I paid ten cents the first time,
but they let me in the second and third times for free.
That was awful kind,
since I didn't have another dime
and I couldn't bring myself to
hand over Ma's book of poetry
from the shelf over the piano.

It was really something to see the oil paintings,
the watercolors,
the pastels and charcoals.
There were pictures of the Panhandle in the old days
with the grass blowing and wolves,
there was a painting of a woman getting dressed
in a room of curtains,
and a drawing of a railroad station
with a garden out the front,
and a sketch of a little girl holding an enormous cat
in her lap.

But now the exhibit is gone,
the paintings
stored away in spare rooms
or locked up
where no one can see them.
I feel such a hunger
to see such things.
And such an anger
because I can't.

December 1934

Winter 1935

State Tests Again

Miss Freeland said
our grade
topped the entire state of Oklahoma
on the state tests again, twenty-four
points higher
than the state average.

Wish I could run home and tell Ma
and see her nod
and hear her say,

"I knew you could."

It would be enough.

January 1935

Christmas Dinner Without the Cranberry Sauce

Miss Freeland
was my ma
at the school
Christmas dinner.

I thought I'd be
the only one
without a
real ma,
but two other motherless girls came.

We served turkey,
chestnut dressing,
sweet potatoes, and brown gravy.
Made it all ourselves
and it came out
pretty good,
better than the Christmas dinner I made for my
father
at home,
where we sat at the table,
silent, just the two of us.

Being there without Ma,
without the baby,

wouldn't have been so bad,
if I'd just remembered the cranberry sauce.
My father loved Ma's special cranberry sauce.
But she never showed me how to make it.

January 1935

Driving the Cows

Dust
piles up like snow
across the prairie,
dunes leaning against fences,
mountains of dust pushing over barns.
Joe De La Flor can't afford to feed his cows,
can't afford to sell them.
County Agent Dewey comes,
takes the cows behind the barn,
and shoots them.
Too hard to
watch their lungs clog with dust,
like our chickens, suffocated.
Better to let the government take them,
than suffer the sight of their bony hides
sinking down
into the earth.

Joe De La Flor
rides the range.
Come spring he'll gather Russian thistle,
pulling the plant while it's still green and young,
before the prickles form, before it breaks free
to tumble across the plains.
He gathers thistle to feed what's left of his cattle,
his bone-thin cattle,

cattle he drives away from the dried-up Beaver River,
to where the Cimarron still runs,
pushing the herd across the breaks,
where they might last another week, maybe two,
until it
rains.

January 1935

First Rain

Sunday night,
I stretch my legs in my iron bed
under the roof.
I place a wet cloth over my nose to keep
from breathing dust
and wipe the grime tracings from around my mouth,
and shiver, thinking of Ma.
I am kept company by the sound of my heart
drumming.

Restless,
I tangle in the dusty sheets,
sending the sand flying,
cursing the grit against my skin,
between my teeth,
under my lids,
swearing I'll leave this forsaken place.

I hear the first drops.
Like the tapping of a stranger
at the door of a dream,
the rain changes everything.
It strokes the roof,
streaking the dusty tin,
ponging,

a concert of rain notes,
spilling from gutters,
gushing through gullies,
soaking into the thirsty earth outside.

Monday morning dawns,
cloaked in mist.
I button into my dress, slip on my sweater,
and push my way off the porch,
sticking my face into the fog,
into the moist skin of the fog.
The sound of dripping surrounds me as I
walk to town.

Soaked to my underwear,
I can't bear to go
through the schoolhouse door,
I want only to stand in the rain.

Monday afternoon,
Joe De La Flor brushes mud from his horse,
Mr. Kincannon hires my father
to pull his Olds out of the muck on Route 64.

And later,
when the clouds lift,
the farmers, surveying their fields,

nod their heads as
the frail stalks revive,
everyone, everything, grateful for this moment,
free of the
weight of dust.

January 1935

Haydon P. Nye

Haydon P. Nye died this week.
I knew him to wave,
he liked the way I played piano.

The newspaper said when Haydon first came
he could see only grass,
grass and wild horses and wolves roaming.

Then folks moved in and sod got busted
and bushels of wheat turned the plains to gold,
and Haydon P. Nye
grabbed the Oklahoma Panhandle in his fist
and held on.

By the time the railroad came in
on land Haydon sold them,
the buffalo and the wild horses had gone.

Some years
Haydon Nye saw the sun dry up his crop,
saw the grasshoppers chew it down,
but then came years of rain
and the wheat thrived,
and his pockets filled,
and his big laugh came easy.

They buried Haydon Nye on his land,
busted more sod to lay down his bones.
Will they sow wheat on his grave,
where the buffalo
once grazed?

January 1935

Scrubbing Up Dust

Walking past the Crystal Hotel
I saw Jim Martin down on his knees.
He was scraping up mud that had
dried to crust
after the rain mixed with dust Sunday last.

When I got home
I took a good look at the steps
and the porch
and the windows.
I saw them with Ma's eyes and thought about
how she'd been haunting me.

I thought about Ma,
who would've washed clothes,
beaten furniture,
aired rugs,
scrubbed floors,
down on her knees,
brush in hand,
breaking that mud
like the farmers break sod,
always watching over her shoulder
for the next duster to roll in.

My stubborn ma,

she'd be doing it all
with my brother Franklin to tend to.
She never could stand a mess.
My father doesn't notice the dried mud.
Least he never tells me,
not that he tells me much of anything these days.
With Ma gone,
if the mud's to be busted,
the job falls to me.
It isn't the work I hate,
the knuckle-breaking work of beating mud out of
every blessed thing,
but every day
my fingers and hands
ache so bad. I think
I should just let them rest,
let the dust rest,
let the world rest.
But I can't leave it rest,
on account of Ma,
haunting.

January 1935

Outlined by Dust

My father stares at me
while I sit across from him at the table,
while I wash dishes in the basin,
my back to him,
the picked and festered bits of my hands in agony.
He stares at me
as I empty the wash water at the roots
of Ma's apple trees.

He spends long days
digging for the electric-train folks
when they can use him,
or working here,
nursing along the wheat,
what there is of it,
or digging the pond.

He sings sometimes under his breath,
even now,
even after so much sorrow.
He sings a man's song,
deep with what has happened to us.
It doesn't swing lightly
the way Ma's voice did,
the way Miss Freeland's voice does,

the way Mad Dog sings.
My father's voice starts and stops,
like a car short of gas,
like an engine choked with dust,
but then he clears his throat
and the song starts up again.

He rubs his eyes
the way I do,
with his palms out.
Ma never did that.
And he wipes the milk from his
upper lip same as me,
with his thumb and forefinger.
Ma never did that, either.

We don't talk much.
My father never was a talker.
Ma's dying hasn't changed that.
I guess he gets the sound out of him with the
songs he sings.

I can't help thinking
how it is for him,
without Ma.
Waking up alone, only
his shape
left in the bed,

outlined by dust.
He always smelled a little like her
first thing in the morning,
when he left her in bed
and went out to do the milking.
She'd scuff into the kitchen a few minutes later,
bleary eyed,
to start breakfast.
I don't think she was ever
really meant for farm life,
I think once she had bigger dreams,
but she made herself over
to fit my father.

Now he smells of dust
and coffee,
tobacco and cows.
None of the musky woman smell left that was Ma.

He stares at me,
maybe he is looking for Ma.
He won't find her.
I look like him,
I stand like him,
I walk across the kitchen floor
with that long-legged walk
of his.
I can't make myself over the way Ma did.

And yet, if I could look in the mirror and see her in
my face.
If I could somehow know that Ma
and baby Franklin
lived on in me . . .

But it can't be.
I'm my father's daughter.

January 1935

114

The President's Ball

All across the land,
couples dancing,
arm in arm, hand in hand,
at the Birthday Ball.

My father puts on his best overalls,
I wear my Sunday dress,
the one with the white collar,
and we walk to town
to the Legion Hall
and join the dance. Our feet flying,
me and my father,
on the wooden floor whirling
to Arley Wanderdale and the Black Mesa Boys.

Till ten,
when Arley stands up from the piano,
to announce we raised thirty-three dollars
for infantile paralysis,
a little better than last year.

And I remember last year,
when Ma was alive and we were
crazy excited about the baby coming.
And I played at this same party for Franklin D.
Roosevelt

and Joyce City
and Arley.

Tonight, for a little while
in the bright hall folks were almost free,
almost free of dust,
almost free of debt,
almost free of fields of withered wheat.
Most of the night I think I smiled.
And twice my father laughed.
Imagine.

January 1935

Lunch

No one's going hungry at school today.
The government
sent canned meat,
rice,
potatoes.
The bakery
sent loaves of bread,
and
Scotty Moore, George Nall, and Willie Harkins
brought in milk,
fresh creamy milk
straight from their farms.
Real lunch and then
stomachs
full and feeling fine
for classes
in the afternoon.

The little ones drank themselves into white
mustaches,
they ate
and ate,
until pushing back from their desks,
their stomachs round,
they swore they'd never eat again.

The older girls,
Elizabeth and LoRaine, helped Miss Freeland
cook,
and Hillary and I,
we served and washed,
our ears ringing with the sound of satisfied children.

February 1935

Guests

In our classroom this morning,
we came in to find a family no one knew.

They were shy,
a little frightened,
embarrassed.
A man and his wife, pretty far along with a baby
coming,

a baby
coming

two little kids
and a grandma.
They'd moved into our classroom during the night.
An iron bed
and some pasteboard boxes. That's all they had.
They'd cleaned the room first, and arranged it,
making a private place for themselves.

"I'm on the look for a job," the man said.
"The dust blew so mean last night
I thought to shelter my family here awhile."

The two little kids turned their big eyes
from Miss Freeland
back to their father.

"I can't have my wife sleeping in the cold truck,
not now. Not with the baby coming so soon."

Miss Freeland said they could stay
as long as they wanted.

February 1935

Family School

Every day we bring fixings for soup
and put a big pot on to simmer.
We share it at lunch with our guests,
the family of migrants who have moved out from dust
and Depression
and moved into our classroom.
We are careful to take only so much to eat,
making sure there's enough soup left in the pot for
their supper.

Some of us bring in toys
and clothes for the children.
I found a few things of my brother's
and brought them to school,
little feed-sack nighties,
so small,
so full of hope.

Franklin
never wore a one of the nighties Ma made him,
except the one we buried him in.

The man, Buddy Williams,
helps out around the school,
fixing windows and doors,
and the bad spot on the steps,

cleaning up the school yard
so it never looked so good.

The grandma takes care of the children,
bringing them out when the dust isn't blowing,
letting them chase tumbleweeds across the field
behind the school,
but when the dust blows,
the family sits in their little apartment inside our
classroom,
studying Miss Freeland's lessons
right alongside us.

February 1935

Birth

One morning when I arrive at school
Miss Freeland says to keep the kids out,
that the baby is coming
and no one can enter the building
until the birthing is done.
I think about Ma
and how that birth went.
I keep the kids out and listen behind me,
praying for the sound of a baby
crying into this world,
and not the silence
my brother brought with him.
And then the cry comes
and I have to go away for a little while
and just walk off the feelings.

Miss Freeland rings the bell to call us in
but I'm not ready to come back yet.
When I do come,
I study how fine that baby girl is. How perfect,
and that she is wearing a feed-sack nightgown that
was my brother's.

February 1935

Time to Go

They left a couple weeks after the baby came,
all of them crammed inside that rusty old truck.
I ran half a mile in their dust to catch them.
I didn't want to let that baby go.
"Wait for me," I cried,
choking on the cloud that rose behind them.
But they didn't hear me.
They were heading west.
And no one was looking back.

February 1935

Something Sweet from Moonshine

Ashby Durwin
and his pal Rush
had themselves a
fine operation on the Cimarron River,
where the water still runs a little,
though the fish are mostly dead
from the dust floating on the surface.
Ashby and Rush were cooking up moonshine
in their giant metal still on the bank
when Sheriff Robertson caught them.
He found jugs of finished whiskey,
and barrels and barrels of mash,
he found two sacks of rye,
and he found sugar,
one thousand pounds of sugar.

The government men took Ashby and Rush off to
Enid
for breaking the law,
but Sheriff Robertson stayed behind,
took apart the still,
washed away the whiskey and the mash,
and thought about that sugar,
all that sugar, one-half ton of sugar.
Sheriff decided
some should find its way

into the mouths of us kids.
Bake for them, Miss Freeland, he said,
bake them cakes and cookies and pies,
cook them custard and cobbler and crisp,
make them candy and taffy and apple pandowdy.

Apple pandowdy!

These kids,
Sheriff Robertson said,
ought to have something sweet to
wash down their dusty milk.
And so we did.

February 1935

Dreams

Each day after class lets out,
each morning before it begins,
I sit at the school piano
and make my hands work.
In spite of the pain,
in spite of the stiffness
and scars.
I make my hands play piano.
I have practiced my best piece over and over
till my arms throb,
because Thursday night
the Palace Theatre is having a contest.
Any man, woman, or child
who sings,
dances,
reads,
or plays worth a lick
can climb onto that stage.
Just register by four P.M.
and give them a taste of what you can do
and you're in,
performing for the crowd,
warming up the audience for the
Hazel Hurd Players.
I figure if I practice enough
I won't shame myself.

And we sure could use the extra cash
if I won.
Three-dollar first prize,
two-dollar second,
one-dollar third.
But I don't know if I could win anything,
not anymore.
It's the playing I want most,
the proving I can still do it.
without Arley making excuses.
I have a hunger,
for more than food.
I have a hunger
bigger than Joyce City.
I want tongues to tie, and
eyes to shine at me
like they do at Mad Dog Craddock.
Course they never will,
not with my hands all scarred up,
looking like the earth itself,
all parched and rough and cracking,
but if I played right enough,
maybe they would see past my hands.
Maybe they could feel at ease with me again,
and maybe then,
I could feel at ease with myself.

February 1935

The Competition

I suppose everyone in Joyce City and beyond,
all the way to Felt
and Keyes
and even Guymon,
came to watch the talent show at the Palace,
Thursday night.

Backstage,
we were seventeen amateur acts,
our wild hearts pounding,
our lips sticking to our teeth,
our urge to empty ourselves
top and bottom,
made a sorry sight
in front of the
famous Hazel Hurd Players.

But they were kind to us,
helped us with our makeup and our hair,
showed us where to stand,
how to bow,
and the quickest route to the
toilet.

The audience hummed on the other side of the
closed curtain,

Ivy Huxford
kept peeking out and giving reports
of who was there,
and how she never saw so many seats
filled in the Palace,
and that she didn't think they could
squeeze a
rattlesnake
into the back
even if he paid full price,
the place was so packed.

My father told me he'd come
once chores were done.
I guess he did.

The Grover boys led us off.
They worked a charm,
Baby on the sax,
Jake on the banjo,
and Ben on the clarinet.
The Baker family followed, playing
just like they do at home
every night after dinner.
They didn't look nervous at all.
The tap dancers,
they rattled the teeth in their jaws
and the eyeballs in their skulls,

their feet flying,
their arms swinging,
their mouths gapping.
Then Sunny Lee Hallem
tumbled and leaped onto the stage,
the sweat flying off her,
spotting the Palace floor.
Marsh Worton struggled out,
his accordion leading the way.
George and Agnes Harkins ran their fingers over the
strings of their harps,
made you want to look up into the heavens for
angels,
but only scenery
and lights
and ropes and sandbags hung overhead,
and then there was me on piano.

I went on somewhere near the backside of middle,
getting more and more jittery with each act,
till my time came.
I played "Bye, Bye, Blackbird"
my own way,
messing with the tempo,
and the first part sounded like
I used just my elbows,
but the middle sounded good
and the end,

I forgot I was even playing
in front of the packed Palace Theatre.
I dropped right inside the music and
didn't feel anything
till after
when the clapping started
and that's when I noticed my hands hurting
straight up to my shoulders.
But the applause
made me forget the pain,
the audience roared when I finished,
they came to their feet,
and I got third prize,
one dollar,
while Mad Dog Craddock, singing,
won second,
and Ben Grover
and his crazy clarinet
took first.

The tap dancers pouted into their mirrors,
peeling off their makeup and their smiles.
Birdie Jasper claimed
it was all my fault she didn't win,
that the judges were just being nice to a cripple,
but the harpin' Harkins were kind
and the Hazel Hurd Players
wrapped their long arms around me

and said I was swell
and in the sweaty dim chaos backstage
I ignored the pain running up and down my arms,
I felt like I was part of something grand.
But they had to give my ribbon and my dollar to my
father,
'cause I couldn't hold
anything in my hands.

February 1935

The Piano Player

Arley says,
"We're
doing a show at the school in a week, Billie Jo.
Come play with us."

If I asked my father
he'd say yes.
It's okay with him if I want to play.
He didn't even know I was at the piano again till the
other night.
He's making some kind of effort to get on
better with me now,
Since I "did him proud" at the Palace.

But I say, "No."

It's too soon after the contest.
It still hurts too much.

Arley doesn't understand.
"Just practice more," he says.
"You'll get it back,
you can travel with us again this summer
if you'd like."

I don't say

it hurts like the parched earth with each note.
I don't say,
one chord and
my hands scream with pain for days.
I don't show him
the swelling
or my tears.

I tell him, "I'll try."

At home, I sit at
Ma's piano,
I don't touch the keys.
I don't know why.

I play "Stormy Weather" in my mind,
following the phrases in my imagination,
saving strength,
so that when I sit down at a piano that is not Ma's,
when everyone crowds into the school
for Arley's show,
no one can say
that Billie Jo Kelby plays like a cripple.

March 1935

No Good

I did play like a cripple at Arley's show,
not that Arley would ever say it.
But my hands are no good anymore,
my playing's no good.
Arley understands, I think.
He won't ask again.

March 1935

Snow

Had to check
yesterday morning
to make sure that was
snow
on the ground,
not dust.
But you can't make a dustball
pack together
and slam against the side of the barn, and
echo across the fields.
So I know
it was snow.

March 1935

Night School

My father thought maybe
he ought to go to night school,
so if the farm failed
there'd be prospects to fall back on.
He's starting to sound like Ma.

"The farm won't fail," I tell him.
"Long as we get some good rain."
I'm starting to sound like him.

"It's mostly ladies in those classes," he says,
"they take bookkeeping and civics,
and something called business English."

I can't imagine him
taking any of those things.
But maybe he doesn't care so much about the classes.
Maybe he's thinking more about the company of
ladies.

I'll bet none of the ladies mind
spending time with my father,
he's still good looking
with his strong back,
and his blondy-red hair
and his high cheeks rugged with wind.

I shouldn't mind either.
It's dinner I don't have to
come up with,
'cause the ladies bring chicken and biscuits for him.
I'm glad to get out of cooking.
Sometimes with my hands,
it's hard to keep the fire,
wash the pans,
hold the knife, and spread a little butter.
But I do mind his spending time with all those
biddies.

I turn my back on him as he goes,
and settle myself in the parlor
and touch Ma's piano.

My fingers leave sighs
in the dust.

March 1935

Dust Pneumonia

Two Fridays ago,
Pete Guymon drove in with a
truck full of produce.
He joked with Calb Hardly,
Mr. Hardly's son,
while they unloaded eggs and cream
down at the store.
Pete Guymon teased Calb Hardly about the Wildcats
losing to Hooker.
Calb Hardly teased Pete Guymon about his wheezy truck
sucking in dust.

Last Friday,
Pete Guymon took ill with dust pneumonia.
Nobody knew how to keep that produce truck on the
road.
It sat,
filled with turkeys and heavy hens
waiting for delivery,
it sat out in front of Pete's drafty shack,
and sits there still,
the cream curdling
the apples going soft.

Because a couple of hours ago,
Pete Guymon died.

Mr. Hardly
was already on the phone to a new produce supplier,
before evening.
He had people in his store
and no food to sell them.

His boy, Calb,
slammed the basketball against the side of the house
until Calb's ma yelled for him to quit,
and late that night a truck rattled up to the store,
with colored springs,
dozens of hens,
filthy eggs,
and a driver with no interest whatsoever in young
Calb Hardly
or his precious Wildcats.

March 1935

Dust Storm

I never would have gone to see the show
if I had known a storm like this would come.
I didn't know when going in,
but coming out
a darker night I'd never seen.
I bumped into a box beside the Palace door
and scraped my shins,
then tripped on something in my path,
I don't know what,
and walked into a phone pole,
bruised my cheek.

The first car that I met was sideways in the road.
Bowed down, my eyes near shut,
trying to keep the dust out,
I saw his headlights just before I reached them.

The driver called me over and I felt my way,
following his voice.
He asked me how I kept the road.
"I feel it with my feet," I shouted over the
roaring wind,
"I walk along the edge.
One foot on the road, one on the shoulder."
And desperate to get home,
he straightened out his car,

and straddled tires on the road and off,
and slowly pulled away.

I kept along. I know that there were others
on the road,
from time to time I'd hear someone cry out,
their voices rose like ghosts on the howling wind;
no one could see. I stopped at neighbors'
just to catch my breath
and made my way from town
out to our farm.
Everyone said to stay
but I guessed
my father would
come out to find me
if I didn't show,
and get himself lost in the
raging dust and maybe die
and I
didn't want that burden on my soul.

Brown earth rained down
from sky.
I could not catch my breath
the way the dust pressed on my chest
and wouldn't stop.
The dirt blew down so thick
it scratched my eyes

and stung my tender skin,
it plugged my nose and filled inside my mouth.
No matter how I pressed my lips together,
the dust made muddy tracks
across my tongue.

But I kept on,
spitting out mud,
covering my mouth,
clamping my nose,
the dust stinging the raw and open
stripes of scarring on my hands,
and after some three hours I made it home.

Inside I found my father's note
that said he'd gone to find me
and if I should get home, to just stay put.
I hollered out the front door
and the back;
he didn't hear,
I didn't think he would.
The wind took my voice and busted it
into a thousand pieces,
so small
the sound
blew out over Ma and Franklin's grave,
thinner than a sigh.

I waited for my father through the night, coughing up
dust,
cleaning dust out of my ears,
rinsing my mouth, blowing mud out of my nose.

Joe De La Flor stopped by around four to tell me
they found one boy tangled in a barbed-wire fence,
another smothered in a drift of dust.

After Joe left I thought of the famous Lindberghs,
and how their baby was killed and never came back
to them.
I wondered if my father would come back.

He blew in around six A.M.
It hurt,
the sight of him
brown with dirt,
his eyes as red as raw meat,
his feet bruised from walking in worn shoes
stepping where he couldn't see
on things that bit and cut into his flesh.

I tried to scare up something we could eat,
but couldn't keep the table clear of dust.
Everything I set
down for our breakfast
was covered before we took a bite,

and so we chewed the grit and swallowed
and I thought of the cattle
dead from mud in their lungs,
and I thought of the tractor
buried up to the steering wheel,
and Pete Guymon,
and I couldn't even recognize the man
sitting across from me,
sagging in his chair,
his red hair gray and stiff with dust,
his face deep lines of dust,
his teeth streaked brown with dust.
I turned the plates and glasses upside down,
crawled into bed, and slept.

March 1935

Broken Promise

It rained
a little
everywhere
but here.

March 1935

Motherless

If Ma could put her arm across my shoulder
sometime,
or stroke back my hair,
or sing me to sleep, making the soft sounds,
the reassuring noises,
that no matter how brittle and sharp life seemed,
no matter how brittle and sharp she seemed,
she was still my ma who loved me,
then I think I wouldn't be so eager to go.

March 1935

Following in His Steps

Haydon Parley Nye's wife,
Fonda,
died today,
two months after she lost her man.

The cause of death was
dust pneumonia,
but I think
she couldn't go on without Haydon.

When Ma died,
I didn't want to go on, either.
I don't know. I don't feel the same now,
not exactly.
Now that I see that one day
comes after another
and you get through them
one measure at a time.
But I'd like to go,
not like Fonda Nye,
I don't want to die,
I just want to go,
away,
out of the dust.

March 1935

Spring 1935

Heartsick

The hard part is in spite of everything
if I had any boy court me,
it'd be Mad Dog Craddock.
But Mad Dog can have any girl.
Why would he want me?

I'm so restless.
My father asks what's going on with me.
I storm up to my room,
leaving him alone
standing in the kitchen.
If Ma was here
she would come up and listen.
And then later,
she would curl beside my father,
and assure him that everything was all right,
and soothe him into his farmer's sleep.

My father and I,
we can't soothe each other.
I'm too young,
he's too old,
and we don't know how to talk anymore
if we ever did.

April 1935

Skin

My father has a raised spot
on the side of his nose
that never was there before
and won't go away.
And there's another on his cheek
and two more on his neck,
and I wonder
why the heck is he fooling around.
He knows what it is.
His father had those spots too.

April 1935

Regrets

I never go by Arley's anymore.
Still,
every week
he comes to school to teach and
sometimes
I bump into Vera, or
Miller Rice,
or Mad Dog.

They are always kind.
They ask after my father.
They ask how my hands are feeling.
I cross my arms in front of me
tight
so my scars won't show.

These days Mad Dog looks at me
halfway between picking a fight and kindness.
He walks with me a ways some afternoons,
never says a word.
He's quiet once the other girls go off.
I've had enough of quiet men.
I ought to keep clear of Mad Dog.
But I don't.

April 1935

Fire on the Rails

I hate fire.
Hate it.
But the entire Oklahoma Panhandle is so dry,
everything is going up in flames.
Everything too ready to ignite.
Last week
the school caught fire.
Damage was light,
on account of it being caught early.
Most kids joked about it next day,
but it terrified me.
I could hardly go back in the building.
And this week
three boxcars
in the train yard
burned to ash.
Jim Goin and Harry Kesler
spotted the fire,
and that was a miracle
considering the fierceness of the dust storm
at the time.
The fire boys
tore over,
but they couldn't put the blaze out without water,
and water is exactly what they didn't have.
So they separated the burning cars

and moved them down a siding,
away from any little thing that might catch
if the flames hopped.
It was all they talked about at school.
The dust blew,
they say,
so you'd think it would have smothered the fire out,
but the flames,
crazy in the wind,
licked away at the wooden frames of the three box
cars,
until nothing remained but warped metal,
and twisted rails,
scorched dirt, and
charred ties.

No one talks about fire
right to my face.
They can't forget how fire changed my life.
But I hear them talking anyway.

April 1935

The Mail Train

They promised
through rain,
heat,
snow,
and gloom
but they never said anything about dust.

And so the mail got stuck
for hours,
for days,
on the Santa Fe
because mountains of dust
had blown over the tracks,
because blizzards of dust
blocked the way.

And all that time,
as the dust beat down on the cars,
a letter was waiting inside a mail bag.
A letter from Aunt Ellis, my father's sister,
written just to me,
inviting me to live with her in Lubbock.
I want to get out of here,
but not to Aunt Ellis,
and not to Lubbock, Texas.
My father didn't say much when I asked

what I should do.
"Let's wait and see,"
he said.
What's that supposed to mean?

April 1935

Migrants

We'll be back when the rain comes,
they say,
pulling away with all they own,
straining the springs of their motor cars.
Don't forget us.

And so they go,
fleeing the blowing dust,
fleeing the fields of brown-tipped wheat
barely ankle high,
and sparse as the hair on a dog's belly.

We'll be back, they say,
pulling away toward Texas,
Arkansas,
where they can rent a farm,
pull in enough cash,
maybe start again.

We'll be back when it rains,
they say,
setting out with their bedsprings and mattresses,
their cookstoves and dishes,
their kitchen tables,
and their milk goats
tied to their running boards

in rickety cages,
setting out for
California,
where even though they say they'll come back,
they just might stay
if what they hear about that place is true.

Don't forget us, they say.
But there are so many leaving,
how can I remember them all?

April 1935

Blankets of Black

On the first clear day
we staggered out of our caves of dust
into the sunlight,
turning our faces to the big blue sky.

On the second clear day
we believed
the worst was over at last.
We flocked outside,
traded in town,
going to stores and coming out
only to find the air still clear
and gentle,
grateful for each easy breath.

On the third clear day
summer came in April
and the churches opened their arms to all comers
and all comers came.
After church,
folks headed for
picnics,
car trips. No one could stay inside.

My father and I argued about the funeral
of Grandma Lucas,

who truly was no relation.
But we ended up going anyway,
driving down the road in a procession to Texhoma.

Six miles out of town the air turned cold,
birds beat their wings
everywhere you looked,
whole flocks
dropping out of the sky,
crowding on fence posts.
I was sulking in the truck beside my father
when
heaven's shadow crept across the plains,
a black cloud,
big and silent as Montana,
boiling on the horizon and
barreling toward us.
More birds tumbled from the sky
frantically keeping ahead of the dust.

We watched as the storm swallowed the light.
The sky turned from blue
to black,
night descended in an instant
and the dust was on us.

The wind screamed.
The blowing dirt ran

so thick
I couldn't see the brim of my hat
as we plunged from the truck,
fleeing.

The dust swarmed
like it had never swarmed before.

My father groped for my hand,
pulled me away from the truck.
We ran,
a blind pitching toward the shelter of a small house,
almost invisible,
our hands tight together,
running toward the ghostly door,
pounding on it with desperation.

A woman opened her home to us,
all of us,
not just me and my father,
but the entire funeral procession,
and one after another,
we tumbled inside, gasping,
our lungs burning for want of air.

All the lamps were lit against the dark,
the house dazed by dust,
gazed weakly out.

The walls shook in the howling wind.
We helped tack up sheets on the windows and doors
to keep the dust down.

Cars and trucks
unable to go on,
their ignitions shorted out by the static electricity,
opened up and let out more passengers,
who stumbled for shelter.
One family came in
clutched together,
their pa, divining the path
with a long wooden rod.

If it hadn't been for the company,
this storm would have broken us
completely,
broken us more thoroughly than
the plow had broken the Oklahoma sod,
more thoroughly than my burns
had broken the ease of my hands.
But for the sake of the crowd,
and the hospitality of the home that sheltered us,
we held on
and waited,
sitting or standing, breathing through wet cloths
as the fog of dust filled the room
and settled slowly over us.

When it let up a bit,
some went on to bury Grandma Lucas,
but my father and I,
we cleaned the thick layer of grime
off the truck,
pulled out of the procession and headed on home,
creeping slowly along the dust-mounded road.

When we got back,
we found the barn half covered in dunes,
I couldn't tell which rise of dust was Ma and
Franklin's grave.
The front door hung open,
blown in by the wind.
Dust lay two feet deep in ripply waves
across the parlor floor,
dust blanketed the cookstove,
the icebox,
the kitchen chairs,
everything deep in dust.
And the piano . . .
buried in dust.

While I started to shovel,
my father went out to the barn.
He came back, and when I asked, he said
the animals
weren't good,

and the tractor was dusted out,
and I said, "It's a wonder
the truck got us home."
I should have held my tongue.
When he tried starting the truck again,
it wouldn't turn over.

April 1935

The Visit

Mad Dog came by
to see how we made out
after the duster.

He didn't come to court me.
I didn't think he had.

We visited more than an hour.
The sky cleared enough to see Black Mesa.
I showed him my father's pond.

Mad Dog said he was going to Amarillo,
to sing, on the radio,
and if he sang good enough,
they might give him a job there.

"You'd leave the farm?" I asked.
He nodded.
"You'd leave school?"
He shrugged.

Mad Dog scooped a handful of dust,
like a boy in a sandpit.
He said, "I love this land,
no matter what."

I looked at his hands.
They were scarless.

Mad Dog stayed longer than he planned.
He ran down the road
back to his father's farm when he realized the time.
Dust rose each place his foot fell,
leaving a trace of him
long after he'd gone.

April 1935

Freak Show

The fellow from Canada,
James Kingsbury,
photographer from the *Toronto Star*,
way up there in Ontario,
the man who took the first pictures of
the Dionne Quintuplets,
left his homeland and
came to Joyce City
looking for some other piece of
oddness,
hoping to photograph the drought
and the dust storms
and
he did
with the help of Bill Rotterdaw
and Handy Poole,
who took him to the sandiest farms and
showed off the boniest cattle in the county.

Mr. Kingsbury's pictures of those Dionne babies
got them famous,
but it also got them taken from their
mother and father
and put on display
like a freak show,
like a tent full of two-headed calves.

Now I'm wondering
what will happen to us
after he finishes taking pictures of our dust.

April 1935

Help from Uncle Sam

The government
is lending us money
to keep the farm going,
money to buy seed,
feed loans for our cow,
for our mule,
for the chickens still alive and the hog,
as well as a little bit of feed
for us.

My father was worried about
paying back,
because of what Ma had said,
but Mrs. Love,
the lady from FERA,
assured him he didn't need to pay a single cent
until the crops came in,
and if the crops never came, then he wouldn't pay a
thing.

So my father said
okay.
Anything to keep going.
He put the paperwork on the shelf,
beside Ma's book of poetry

and the invitation from Aunt Ellis.
He just keeps that invitation from her,
glowering down at me from the shelf above the piano.

April 1935

Let Down

I was invited to graduation,
to play the piano.

I couldn't play.
It had been too long.
My hands wouldn't work.
I just sat on the piano bench,
staring down at the keys.
Everyone waited.
When the silence went on so long
folks started to whisper,
Arley Wanderdale lowered his head and
Miss Freeland started to cry.
I don't know,
I let them down.

I didn't cry.
Too stubborn.
I got up and walked off the stage.

I thought maybe if my father ever went to Doc Rice
to do something about the spots on his skin,
Doc could check my hands too,
tell me what to do about them.

But my father isn't going to Doc Rice,
and now
I think we're both turning to dust.

May 1935

Hope

It started out as snow,
oh,
big flakes
floating
softly,
catching on my sweater,
lacy on the edges of my sleeves.

Snow covered the dust,
softened the
fences,
soothed the parched lips
of the land.

And then it changed,
halfway between snow and rain,
sleet,
glazing the earth.

Until at last
it slipped into rain,
light as mist.

It was the kindest
kind of rain
that fell.

Soft and then a little heavier,
helping along
what had already fallen
into the
hard-pan
earth
until it
rained,
steady as a good friend
who walks beside you,
not getting in your way,
staying with you through a hard time.

And because the rain came
so patient and slow at first,
and built up strength as the earth
remembered how to yield,
instead of washing off,
the water slid in,
into the dying ground
and softened its stubborn pride,
and eased it back toward life.

And then,
just when we thought it would end,
after three such gentle days,
the rain
came

slamming down,
tons of it,
soaking into the ready earth
to the primed and greedy earth,
and soaking deep.

It kept coming,
thunder booming,
lightning
kicking,
dancing from the heavens
down to the prairie,
and my father
dancing with it,
dancing outside in the drenching night
with the gutters racing,
with the earth puddled and pleased,
with my father's near-finished pond filling.

When the rain stopped,
my father splashed out to the barn,
and spent
two days and two nights
cleaning dust out of his tractor,
until he got it running again.
In the dark, headlights shining,
he idled toward the freshened fields,

certain the grass would grow again,
certain the weeds would grow again,
certain the wheat would grow again too.

May 1935

The Rain's Gift

The rain
has brought back some grass
and the ranchers
have put away the
feed cake
and sent their cattle
out to graze.
Joe De La Flor
is singing in his saddle again.

May 1935

Hope Smothered

While I washed up dinner dishes in the pan,
the wind came from the west
bringing—
dust.
I'd just stripped all the gummed tape from the
windows.
Now I've got dust all over the clean dishes.

I can hardly make myself
get started cleaning again.

Mrs. Love is taking applications
for boys to do CCC work.
Any boy between eighteen and twenty-eight can join.
I'm too young
and the wrong sex
but what I wouldn't give to be
working for the CCC
somewhere far from here,
out of the dust.

May 1935

Sunday Afternoon at the Amarillo Hotel

Everybody gathered at
the Joyce City Hardware and Furniture Company
on Sunday
to hear Mad Dog Craddock
sing on WDAG
from the Amarillo Hotel.
They hooked up speakers
and the sweet sound
of Mad Dog's voice
filled the creaky aisles.

Arley Wanderdale was in Amarillo with Mad Dog,
singing and playing the piano,
and the Black Mesa Boys were there
too.
I ached for not being there with them.

But there was nothing more most folks in Joyce City
wanted to do
than spend a half hour
leaning on counters,
sitting on stairs,
resting in chairs,
staring at the hardware
and the tableware,
listening to hometown boys

making big-time music
on the radio.

They kept time in the aisles,
hooting after each number,
and when Mad Dog finished his last song, they sent
the dust swirling,
cheering and whooping,
patting each other on the back,
as if they'd been featured
on WDAG themselves.

I tried cheering for Mad Dog with everyone else,
but my throat
felt like a trap had
snapped down on it.

That Mad Dog, he didn't have
a thing to worry about.
He sang good, all right.
He'll go far as he wants.

May 1935

Baby

Funny thing about babies.
Ma died having one,
the Lindberghs said good night to one and lost it,
and somebody
last Saturday
decided to
give one away.

Reverend Bingham says
that Harley Madden
was sweeping the dust out of church,
shining things up for Sunday service,
when he swept himself up to a package
on the north front steps.

He knelt,
studying the parcel,
and called to Reverend Bingham,
who came right by and opened the package up.

It held a living baby.
Reverend Bingham took it to Doc Rice.
Doc checked it, said it was fine,
only small,
less than a five-pound sack of sugar,

and a little cold from
spending time on the north front steps,
but Mrs. Bingham
and the reverend
warmed that baby with
blankets and sugar water,
and tender talk,
and the whole of Joyce City came forward with gifts.

I asked my father if we could adopt it,
but he said
we stood about as much chance
of getting that baby
as the wheat stood of growing,
since we couldn't give the baby anything
not even a ma.
Then he looked at me
sorry as dust.
And to make up for it,
he pulled out a box with the rest of the clothes
Ma had made for our new baby
and told me to drop them by the church if I wanted.

I found the dimes Ma'd been saving,
my earnings from the piano,
inside an envelope,
in the box of baby Franklin's nighties.

She had kept those dimes to send me
to Panhandle A and M.
To study music.

No point now.

I sat at her piano a long time after I
got back from the church,
imagining
a song for my little brother,
buried in Ma's arms on a knoll overlooking the
banks of the Beaver,
imagining a song for the Lindbergh baby
stiff in the woods,
imagining a song for this new baby
who
would not be my father's son.

May 1935

Old Bones

Once
dinosaurs roamed
in Cimarron County.
Bones
showing
in the green shale,
ribs the size of plow blades,
hip bones like crank phones,
and legs running
like fence rails
down to a giant
foot.

A chill shoots up my spine
imagining a dinosaur
slogging out of an Oklahoma sea,
with turtles swimming around its legs.
I can see it sunning itself on the swampy banks,
beyond it a forest of ferns.
It's almost easy to imagine,
gazing out from our house
at the dust-crushed fields,
easy to imagine filling in all the emptiness with green,
easy to imagine such a beast
brushing an itchy rump against our barn.
But all that remains of it

is bone,
broken and turned to stone,
trapped in the hillside,
this once-upon-a-time real-live dinosaur
who lived,
and fed,
and roamed
like a ridiculous
long-necked cow,
and then fell down and died.
I think for a moment of Joe De La Flor
herding brontosaurus instead of cattle
and I
smile.

I tell my father,
Let's go to the site
and watch the men chip away with ice picks,
let's see how they plaster the bones.
Please, before they ship the whole thing to Norman.

I am thinking
that a dinosaur is getting out of Joyce City
a hundred million years too late to
appreciate the trip,
and that I ought to get out before my own
bones turn to stone.

But I keep my thoughts to myself.

My father thinks awhile,
rubbing that spot on his neck.
He looks out the window,
out across the field,
toward the knoll where Ma and the baby lie.
"It's best to let the dead rest," he says.
And we stay home.

June 1935

Summer 1935

The Dream

Piano, my silent
                    mother,
                            I can touch you,
you are cool
                    and smooth
                            and willing
to stay with me
                    stay with me
                            talk to me.
Uncomplaining
                    you accept
                            the cover to your keys
and still
                    you
                            make room
for all that I
                    place
                            there.

We close our eyes
                    together
                            and together find that stillness
like a pond
                    a pond
                            when the wind is quiet
and the surface

        glazes

                gazing unblinking

at the blue sky.

        I play songs

                that have only the pattern

of my self in them

        and you hum along

                supporting me.

You are the

        companion

                to myself.

The mirror

        with my mother's eyes.

July 1935

Midnight Truth

I am so filled with bitterness,
it comes from the dust, it comes
from the silence of my father, it comes
from the absence of Ma.

I could've loved her better.
She could've loved me, too.
But she's rock and dust and wind now,
she's carved stone,
she's holding my stone brother.

I have given my father so many chances
to understand, to
reach out, to
love me. He once did.
I remember his smile,
his easy talk.
Now there's nothing easy between us.
Sometimes he takes notice of me,
like coming after me in the dust.
But mostly I'm invisible.
Mostly I'm alone.

My father's digging his own grave,
he calls it a pond,
but I know what he's up to.

He is rotting away,
like his father,
ready to leave me behind in the dust.
Well, I'm leaving first.

July 1935

Out of the Dust

This is not a dream.
There's no comfort in dreams.
I try to contain the ache as I leave my bed,
I try to still my heart as I
slip from my room with my kerchief of dimes.
Moving slowly down the stairs,
I cross through the kitchen, taking only some
biscuits,
and leave my father's house.
It's the middle of the night and I hear every sound
inside me, outside me.
I go,
knowing that I'll die if I stay,
that I'm slowly, surely
smothering.

I walk through the calm night,
under the stars.
I walk to
where the train stops long enough
for a long-legged girl to latch on
and as my heart races
I feel the earth tremble beneath me and then
the sound of sharp knives,
metal against metal,
as the train pulls up to the station.

Once I might've headed east,
to Mr. Roosevelt.
Now I slip under cover of darkness
inside a boxcar
and let the train carry me west.
Out of the dust.

August 1935

Gone West

I am stiff and sore.
In two endless days on this train, I have
burned in the desert,
shivered in the mountains,
I have seen the
camps of dust-bowl migrants
along the tracks.

There was one girl.
I saw her through the slat in the boxcar.
She stared up at the passing train.
She stood by the tracks watching,
and I knew her.

August 1935

Something Lost, Something Gained

He climbs into my car.
He's dirty and he has a sour smell.
His eyes are ringed by the soil that comes from riding
trains.
But there's a deeper shadow to those eyes,
like ashes,
like death.
He needs a hair comb and a shave,
and a mending needle applied to his pants.

He speaks to me,
"Where you from, miss?" he wants to know.
He shows me a picture of his family.
A wife. Three boys.
The photograph is all he carries.
That and the shredding, stinking clothes on his back.
I feed him two of the stale biscuits I've been hoarding
and save the rest.
I'll be hungry tonight,
what with giving my day's biscuits away.
But I can see the gaunt of hunger in his cheeks.
He asks if I have water and I shake my head,
my tongue thick with thirst.
He eats the biscuits.
He doesn't care they're caked with dust.

He finishes eating and crumbs stick to his mustache.
He's staring hard at me and his eyes water.
"I've done it again," he says.
"Taken food from a child."
I show him my cloth bag with more biscuits.
"At home," he said, "I couldn't feed them,
couldn't stand the baby always crying.
And my wife,
always that dark look following me.
Couldn't take no more.

Lost our land, they tractored us out so's we had to
leave,
rented awhile, then moved in with Lucille's kin.
Couldn't make nothing grow."

I nodded. "I know."

We talked as the train rocked,
as the cars creaked,
as the miles showed nothing but empty space,
we talked through the pink of the setting sun,
and into the dark.
I told him about Ma dying.
I told him about my father,
and how the thing that scared us both the most
was being left alone.

And now I'd gone and left him.
I told him about the piano,
and Arley Wanderdale,
and how I wasn't certain of the date,
but I thought it might be my birthday,
but he was sleeping by then, I think.

He was like tumbleweed.
Ma had been tumbleweed too,
holding on for as long as she could,
then blowing away on the wind.

My father was more like the sod.
Steady, silent, and deep.
Holding on to life, with reserves underneath
to sustain him, and me,
and anyone else who came near.
My father
stayed rooted, even with my tests and my temper,
even with the double sorrow of
his grief and my own,
he had kept a home
until I broke it.

When I woke,
the man was gone, and so were my biscuits,
but under my hat I found the photograph of his
family,

the wife and three boys.
Maybe the photograph was
left in trade for the biscuits,
maybe it was a birthday gift,
the one thing he had left to give.
The children in the picture were clean and serious,
looking out with a certain longing.
The baby had his eyes.
On the back of the photograph,
in pencil,
was the address of his family in
Moline, Kansas.
First chance, I'd send the picture back,
let his wife know he was still alive.

I got off the train in Flagstaff, Arizona.
A lady from a government agency saw me.
She gave me water and food.
I called Mr. Hardly from her office and asked him to
let my father know . . .
I was coming home.

August 1935

Homeward Bound

Getting away,
it wasn't any better.
Just different.
And lonely.
Lonelier than the wind.
Emptier than the sky.
More silent than the dust,
piled in drifts between me
and my
father.

August 1935

Met

My father is waiting at the station
and I call him
Daddy
for the first time
since Ma died,
and we walk home,
together,
talking.
I tell him about getting out of the dust
and how I can't get out of something
that's inside me.
I tell him he is like the sod,
and I am like the wheat,
and I can't grow everywhere,
but I can grow here,
with a little rain,
with a little care,
with a little luck.
And I tell him how scared I am about those spots on
his skin
and I see he's scared too.
"I can't be my own mother," I tell him,
"and I can't be my own father
and if you're both going to leave me,
well,
what am I supposed to do?"

And when I tell Daddy so,
he promises to call Doc Rice.

He says the pond is done.
We can swim in it once it fills,
and he'll stock it with fish too,
catfish, that I can go out and
catch of an evening
and fry up.
He says I can even plant flowers,
if I want.

As we walk together,
side by side,
in the swell of dust,
I am forgiving him, step by step,
for the pail of kerosene.
As we walk together,
side by side,
in the sole-deep dust,
I am forgiving myself
for all the rest.

August 1935

Autumn 1935

Cut It Deep

I went in with Daddy to see Doc Rice.
Doc said,
"Why'd you wait so long
to show someone those spots, Bayard?"
I scowled at Daddy.
He looked at the wall.
I think
he didn't care much,
if he had some cancer
and took and died.
Figured he'd see Ma then,
he'd see my brother.
It'd be out of his hands.
He'd be out of the dust.

Now he's going to wear bandages
where Doc cut the cancer out
the best he could.
And we have to wait
and hope Daddy didn't
get help too late.

I ask Doc about my hands.
"What," I say,
"can I do with them?"
Doc looks carefully at the mottled skin,

the stretched and striped and crackled skin.
"Quit picking at them," he says.
"Rub some ointment in them before you go to bed,"
he says.
"And use them, Billie Jo," he says.
"They'll heal up fine if you just use them."

Daddy sits on my bed
and I open the boxes,
the two boxes
that have been in my closet
for years now.
The dust is over everything,
but I blow it off,
and Daddy is so quiet
when he sees
some of the things
that're still so strong of Ma,
and we end up keeping everything but a palmful
of broken doll dishes.
I thought once to go through these boxes with
Ma,
but Daddy is
sitting on the edge of my bed.
My mouth feels cottony.
I fix dinner
and Daddy tells me about
when he was a boy.

He says, "I wasn't always sure
about the wheat,
about the land,
about life in the Panhandle.
I dreamed of running off too,
though I never did.
I didn't have half your sauce, Billie Jo," he says.
And it's the first time I ever knew
there was so much to the two of us,
so much more than our red hair
and our long legs
and the way we rub our eyes
when we're tired.

October 1935

The Other Woman

Her name is Louise,
she stayed by Daddy the days I was away.

The first time I met her she came to dinner bringing two
baskets of food.
She's a good cook
without showing off.

She has a way of making my father do things.
When Louise came to dinner,
Daddy got up and cleaned the kitchen when we were
done eating.
He tied an apron around his middle
and he looked silly as a cow
stuck in a hole,
but Louise ignored that,
and I took a lesson from her.

We walked around the farm
even though she'd probably already seen it
while I was gone.
She didn't ask to be taken to my favorite places,
the loft in the barn,
the banks of the Beaver,
the field where you can
see Black Mesa on a clear day.

She told me
she knew Daddy and I had a history before her,
and she wished she'd been there for the whole thing,
but she wasn't and there wasn't anything to do
but get over it and get on.

We both stared in wonder
at the pond my daddy made
and she said,
a hole like that says a lot about a man.

I didn't intend to, but I liked her,
because she was so plain and so honest,
and because she made Daddy laugh,
and me, too, just like that,
and even though I didn't know
if there was room for her
in me, I could see there was room for her in Daddy.
When I asked him if he wanted me
to go off to Aunt Ellis after all,
Daddy said he hadn't ever wanted it,
he said I was his own and he didn't like to
think about what Aunt Ellis might do with me.
And we laughed, picturing me and Aunt Ellis
together,
and it wasn't a nice laugh, but it was
Aunt Ellis we were talking about after all.

The thing about Louise,
I'll just have to watch how things go and hope
she doesn't crowd me out of Daddy's life, not now,
when I am just finding my way back into it.

October 1935

Not Everywhere

I walk with Daddy
up the slope and look out over the Beaver River.
Louise is back at the house.
She wanted to come
but this is Ma's place,
Ma's grave,
Franklin's too,
and Louise has no business here.
She wants to come everywhere with us.
Well, I won't let her.
Not everywhere.

Daddy says,
"She could have come.
There's room enough for everyone, Billie Jo."
But there's not.
She can come into Ma's kitchen.
She can hang around the barn.
She can sit beside Daddy when he drives the truck.
But Ma's bones are in this hill,
Ma's and Franklin's.
And their bones wouldn't like it,
if Louise came walking up here between us.

October 1935

My Life, or What I Told Louise
After the Tenth Time She Came to Dinner

"I may look like Daddy, but I have my mother's
hands.
Piano hands, Ma called them,
sneaking a look at them any chance she got.
A piano is a grand thing," I say.
"Though ours is covered in dust now.
Under the grime it's dark brown,
like my mother's eyes."

I think about the piano
and how above it hangs a mirror
and to either side of that mirror,
shelves,
where Ma and Daddy's wedding picture once stood,
though Daddy has taken that down.

"Whenever she could,
Ma filled a bowl with apples," I tell Louise.
"I'm crazy about apples,
and she filled a jar with wildflowers when she
found them,
and put them on that shelf above the piano."

On the other shelf Ma's book of poetry remains.
And the invitation from Aunt Ellis,

or what's left of it.
Daddy and I tore it into strips
to mark the poems we thought Ma liked best.

"We weren't always happy," I tell Louise.
"But we were happy enough
until the accident.
When I rode the train west,
I went looking for something,
but I didn't see anything wonderful.
I didn't see anything better than what I already had.
Home."

I look straight into Louise's face.
Louise doesn't flinch.
She looks straight back.
I am the first one to back down.

"My hands don't look real pretty anymore.
But they hardly hurt. They only ache a little,
sometimes.
I could play right now,
maybe,
if I could get the dust out of the piano,
if I wanted to get the dust out of the piano.
But I don't. I'm not ready yet."

And what I like best about her,

is Louise doesn't say what I should do.
She just nods.
And I know she's heard everything I said,
and some things I didn't say too.

November 1935

November Dust

The wheat is growing
even though dust
blows in sometimes.

I walk with Daddy around the farm
and see that
the pond is holding its own,
it will keep Ma's apple trees alive,
nourish her garden,
help the grass around it grow,
enough to lie in and dream
if I feel like it,
and stand in,
and wait for Mad Dog
when he comes past once a week
on his way from Amarillo,
where he works for the radio.

And as long as the
dust doesn't crush
the winter wheat,
we'll have something to show in the spring
for all Daddy's hard work.
Not a lot, but more than last year.

November 1935

Thanksgiving List

Prairie birds, the whistle of gophers, the wind
blowing,
the smell of grass
and spicy earth,
friends like Mad Dog, the cattle down in the river,
water washing over their hooves,
the sky so
big, so full of
shifting clouds,
the cloud shadows creeping
over the fields,
Daddy's smile,
and his laugh,
and his songs,
Louise,
food without dust,
Daddy seeing to Ma's piano,
newly cleaned and tuned,
the days when my hands don't hurt at all,
the thank-you note from Lucille in Moline, Kansas,
the sound of rain,
Daddy's hole staying full of water
as the windmill turns,
the smell of green,
of damp earth,
of hope returning to our farm.

The poppies set to
bloom on Ma and Franklin's grave,
the morning with the whole day waiting,
full of promise,
the night
of quiet, of no expectations, of rest.
And the certainty of home, the one I live in,
and the one
that lives in me.

November 1935

Music

I'm getting to know the music again.
And it is getting to know me.
We sniff each other's armpits,
and inside each other's ears,
and behind each other's necks.
We are both confident, and a little sassy.

And I know now that all the time I was trying to get
out of the dust,
the fact is,
what I am,
I am because of the dust.
And what I am is good enough.
Even for me.

November 1935

Teamwork

Louise and I take walks after dinner
every time she comes.
By the time we get back
the kitchen looks pretty good,
Daddy only leaves a few things he doesn't
understand,
like big pans,
and wooden spoons,
and leftovers,
and that makes me a little irritated
but mostly it makes me love him.
And Louise, knowing exactly what's left to be done,
helps me finish up.

She was my father's teacher at the night school class.
She never married.
She went to college for two years
and studied and worked,
and didn't notice how lonely she was
until she met Daddy and fell into the
big hurt of his eyes.
She knows how to keep a home,
she knows how to cook,
she knows how to make things
last through winters
and drought.

She knows how to smooth things between two
redheaded people.
And she knows how to come into a home
and not step on the toes of a ghost.
I still feel grateful she didn't make cranberry sauce
last month, at the first Thanksgiving we
spent together.
Louise made sweet potatoes and green beans,
and turkey, and two pies, pumpkin
and chocolate.
I was so full
my lids
sighed shut and Daddy walked with Louise instead of
me
out to Ma and Franklin's grave,
where he let Ma know his intentions.
And Ma's bones didn't object.
Neither did mine.

And when they came back to the house,
Daddy still cleaned the kitchen.

December 1935

Finding a Way

Daddy
started talking
about planting
the rest of the acres in wheat,
but then said, No,
let's just go with what we've got right now.

And I've
been playing
a half hour
every day,
making the skin stretch,
making the scars stretch.

The way I see it, hard times aren't only
about money,
or drought,
or dust.
Hard times are about losing spirit,
and hope,
and what happens when dreams dry up.

The tractor's busted,
we don't have the cash to fix it,
but there's nothing saying Daddy can't do the work
by hand.

It can't be any harder than digging a hole
forty by sixty by six feet deep.

Daddy bought a second mule with Louise's help.
Her betrothal gift to him.
He walks behind the team,
step by step, listing the fields to fight the wind.
Maybe the tractor lifted him above the land,
maybe the fields didn't know him anymore,
didn't remember the touch of his feet,
or the stroke of his hand,
or the bones of his knees,
and why should wheat grow for a stranger?
Daddy said he'd try some sorghum,
maybe some cotton,
admitting as how there might be something
to this notion of diversification folks were
talking about,
and yes, he'd bring the grass back
like Ma wanted,
where he wasn't planting anything else.
He'd make new sod.
And I'm learning, watching Daddy, that you can stay
in one place
and still grow.

I wipe dust out of the roasting pan,
I wipe dust off Ma's dishes,

and wait for Daddy to drive in with Louise,
hoping she'll stay a little later,
a little longer,
waiting for the day when she stays for good.

She wears a comical hat, with flowers,
in December,
and when she smiles,
her face is
full enough of springtime, it makes
her hat seem just right.
She brings apples in a sack,
perfect apples she arranges
in a bowl on the shelf,
opposite the book of poetry.
Sometimes, while I'm at the piano,
I catch her reflection in the mirror,
standing in the kitchen, soft-eyed, while Daddy
finishes chores,
and I stretch my fingers over the keys,
and I play.

December 1935

SCHOLASTIC INC
555 Broadwa
New York, N
10012-399

Dear Teacher,

From the first time I encountered the character of Billie Jo
in Karen Hesse's novel *Out of the Dust*, I knew I had met
someone unforgettable. By general description, *Out of the
Dust* sounded like a tough read: a historical novel set
during the 1930s in the Oklahoma dust bowl, written in first
person free verse? But what I found was an absolutely
accessible, readable story about a family torn apart by
tragedy, put back together by forgiveness—and, through it
all, the stirring example of a girl facing the worst in herself
to get to her best.

Scholastic is proud to publish Karen Hesse and especially
honored to have our first Newbery Medal be *Out of the
Dust*. There is so much in this book to inspire and teach
young readers. I am pleased to present this special teacher's
edition of *Out of the Dust* to you and your students.

Sincerely,

Jean Feiwel
Publisher
Scholastic, Inc.

SCHOLASTIC

DISCUSSION AND STUDY GUIDE TO:

Out

of the

Dust

KAREN HESSE

- 1998 Newbery Medal

- 1998 Scott O'Dell Award for Historical Fiction

- An ALA Notable Children's Book

- An ALA Best Book for Young Adults

About the Book

Daddy came in,/ he sat across from Ma and blew his nose./ Mud streamed out./ He coughed and spit out/ mud./ If he had cried,/ his tears would have been mud too,/ but he didn't cry./ And neither did Ma.

In this powerful historical novel, a young teenager named Billie Jo Kelby describes her life from the winter of 1934 through the autumn of 1935. Through her story, readers see what life in the dust bowl was like as Oklahoma farmers struggled to raise crops choked by continual dust storms and families struggled to survive.

Billie Jo and her parents face these hard times together, and despite the never-ending dust, Billie Jo is happy. More than anything, Billie Jo loves to play the piano, and she has begun earning money performing. Ma and Pa are happy, too — soon Ma will give birth, and at last Billie Jo will have a brother or sister.

Then a terrible accident changes everything. Ma mistakes a pail of kerosene that Pa had left next to the stove for water and begins to use it to cook. Fire erupts. After her mother runs outside, Billie Jo tosses the flaming kerosene out the door, realizing too late that Ma is standing right in the path of the fiery liquid. Billie Jo tries desperately to save Ma, beating out the flames with her own hands. Ma and the baby both die, the town gossips that Billie Jo caused the accident, Pa withdraws into a deep depression, and Billie Jo's hands are so badly burned that she cannot play the piano and daily chores are agony.

For a long time, she can forgive neither her father nor herself. She even runs away on a freight train. As she leaves the dust of Oklahoma behind, Billie Jo comes to understand herself and her father in a new way. She returns home; the many hardships she has faced — her mother's tragic death, her father's retreat into depression, her own need to escape, and the personal journey that finally results in healing and forgiveness — all lead Billie Jo "out of the dust" in a most surprising way.

Pre-Reading Activity

UNDERSTANDING TIME AND PLACE

Out of the Dust is an unflinching portrait of life in a time and place in which people faced terrible hardships. The dust storms and the economic disaster that the characters face are very real. Have students share what they already know about the Depression and the dust bowl. If needed, supply some basic facts, including the information that by the 1930s the soil in Oklahoma and neighboring states had become loose and dry partly as the result of converting too much wild grass- land to farmland. Wheat crops failed, and nearly fifty million acres were severely damaged before conservation measures helped put an end to the storms that threatened the lives of people and animals as well as crops. Have students brainstorm what it might have been like to live during that time. How would everyday life be affected?

Discussing the Book

ANALYZING PLOT AND CHARACTER

Early Influences: Two women who are important to Billie Jo are her mother and her teacher, Miss Freeland. Describe these characters. What are some of the important things Billie Jo learns from them?

A Defining Incident: Sometimes, one event can help readers learn a great deal about the characters in the book. After meeting the man in the boxcar, Billie Jo turns around and returns home. What was this man like? How did meeting him affect Billie Jo? In what ways is Billie Jo's father different from this man?

Change: In one year, Billie Jo grows and changes a great deal. Have students review each of the seven main sections of the book. What are Billie Jo's main concerns in each section? How is Billie Jo the same in each section? How does she change? If Billie Jo were to describe herself in 1936, how might her life be different? How would it most likely be the same?

Acts of Courage: Billie Jo and others face many grave difficulties in this story. In your opinion, which character in this story shows the greatest courage? What does he or she do?

THE AUTHOR'S CRAFT

Blank Verse: The author made an unusual choice when she elected to write this novel as a series of short poems told from the point of view of the main character. In what ways does this format help readers get into the story and understand the main character?

Historical Fiction: The author did a great deal of research on life in the dust bowl to help her create authentic setting, events, and characters. Skim through the book for details that seem to reflect facts. What are the most interesting facts you learned about the setting, everyday life in the 1930s?

Theme: Forgiveness: What does it take to be able to forgive? Karen Hesse has said that every relationship in the book — not only the relationships between the people but also the relationships between the people and the land — is about forgiveness. How does Billie Jo show that she has forgiven her father and herself? How does her father show that he has for-given her, himself, and the land? How does the author suggest that in some ways the land also has forgiven the people for misusing it?

Title: Karen Hesse is an author who chooses every word with care. The phrase "out of the dust" appears several times in the book. At one point Billie Jo wants to escape "out of the dust" but later she says, "I can't get out of something that is inside me." How does the title of the book reflect on Billie Jo as a person? How does it reflect on the general experience of people at that time?

Writing Prompts

POETIC PORTRAIT

Have students reread the first entry of the book, the poem *Beginning: August 1920*, and suggest that students use it as a model to create a portrait of themselves or another person. The portrait can describe such things as how or where the person was born, what they look like, and what they like to do. Note the way Karen Hesse uses similes, comparisons with *like* or *as* (e.g., "cheekbones like bicycle handles," "mean as a rattler"), in her poem. Encourage students to use their own similes in the poems they write. The completed portraits may be illustrated with photos and compiled into a class book or displayed on a bulletin board.

NEWSPAPER ARTICLE

To help her learn about daily life in the dust bowl in the 1930s, Karen Hesse spent months reading articles from a newspaper published in the Oklahoma Panhandle during that period. She has said that many of the incidents in the book, especially those related to talent shows, dances, and daily acts of kindness and generosity, are based on events reported in that paper. Invite students to select an event from *Out of the Dust* and retell it in the form of a newspaper article. Before writing, students can examine articles from a local paper for style and structure. Remind students that newspaper articles are concise and answer the questions Who, What, When, Where, and Why.

ESSAY

Despite the terrible hardships they faced, Billie Jo, her family, and their neighbors still found ways to help others who were in need. Ask students to recall these acts of generosity. Which stands out in their minds as the most generous? Why? You may wish to have students create a chart to help them organize their thoughts and recall details to support their opinion before they write. In one column they can describe what help was given; in a second column they can list the reasons that the person who received help needed aid and what might have happened if he or she had not received the help; in a third column they can record information about the person(s) who provided the help, what they gave up, and how they felt after their generous act.

Activities Across the Curriculum

LANGUAGE ARTS

Dramatic Reading: The form of the novel — a series of first person, free verse poems — is unusual. Discuss how this form adds to the atmosphere of the book and the reader's understanding of Billie Jo, the narrator. Read aloud the short poem *Breaking Drought* (February 1934), inviting students to note how the author uses repetition, line breaks, and punctuation to create a rhythm and mood for the poem. Notice especially how the last three lines of the poem are very short and seem to die away, like the few drops of rain that soon disappear. Have students work independently or in small groups to select another poem from the book to read aloud for the class.

Dialogue: The entire story is told from Billie Jo's point of view. What might Billie Jo's father say about the accident if he spoke for himself? Have pairs of students work together to create and act out a dialogue between Billie Jo and her father. First have students write a short scene that takes place shortly after the accident, then have them write another scene that tells how each character feels about the accident toward the end of the book. Invite students to perform their dialogues for the class and have other students comment on the main differences between the two scenes.

Poster: The talent show and the President's ball were events that Billie Jo and her whole community enjoyed. Ask students to skim through the book for descriptions of these events and then select one and create a poster to advertise it. After the posters are complete, students can present them to the class, explaining why they chose the wording and art they used.

SOCIAL STUDIES

Time Line: In addition to dealing with the dust bowl, Billie Jo's father faced hardships when he served as a soldier in World War I. Have students research important events that span the years 1917 through 1935. Then ask students to select ten key events and create a time line to present them in chronological order.

President Franklin D. Roosevelt and the Depression: Throughout the book, Billie Jo makes it clear that President Roosevelt is someone she considers a hero. Have students read about Roosevelt, emphasizing the things he did before he became President and during his first term. Ask students to use the facts they find to write a short essay describing Roosevelt and telling what they think was his greatest accomplishment during that time.

Geography: Have students use an encyclopedia and maps to find answers to the following questions about the dust bowl: Which states were affected? How far did the dust storms travel? In which years did the worst storms occur? Have there been other, more recent dust storms? You may wish to have students use what they discover to create a fact sheet on the dust bowl that can be given to other students before they read *Out of the Dust.*

SCIENCE AND MATH

Ecological Chain Reaction: Entwined with the human stories told in the book, *Out of the Dust* also tells the all too real story of the sequence of events that led to the erosion of the soil, affecting the water cycle and creating dust storms and ecological disaster. Review with students that when the wild grassland or sod was plowed up for farming wheat, the soil became more exposed and vulnerable to erosion, could not hold water as well, and lost important minerals. For an introduction to understanding the dust bowl, read the poem *The Path of Our Sorrow* (September 1934). Have groups work together, using facts from the book and additional resources, to create a diagram that shows the chain of events that led to the dust storms and measures that helped the storms end. Have students present their findings and discuss what lessons we can learn from the dust bowl.

Radio: Mad Dog sings on the radio. By 1934, the radio was a popular fixture in many homes. Invite students to research the development of this invention and its uses and to write a paragraph to summarize what they find out.

Money: Billie Jo's mother gives her fifty cents to buy ingredients for a birthday cake, and she returns home with too much change. As she walks back to the store she thinks about the sheet music she could buy if the extra pennies were hers to spend. Have students visit a local store to research how much money they would have to spend today to bake a birthday cake. If you have access to newspapers or magazines from the 1930s via the Internet or microfiche, have students search for old ads that will give them more information about what things cost in 1934 and how the cost of things has changed. Discuss the reasons prices have changed over the years.

THE ARTS

Music: Billie Jo loves the piano, and she mentions some of the popular songs she plays. Invite students to research the popular music and musicians of the era. If possible, have students bring in tapes or CDs and listen to the music. Students who are able to read music and play an instrument can be encouraged to learn some pieces and perform them.

Art: Each poem in the book creates a strong mood and is rich in visual images. Ask students to select a favorite poem and create a drawing, painting, or collage that reflects the mood and images that the poem suggests.

Film: Bring in the classic film *The Grapes of Wrath* or another film available on video that reflects the life of people during the 1930s. Have students create a chart to compare the characters in the film with the characters in *Out of the Dust.* How are they alike? How are they different?

Discussion guide written by Kylene Beers and Teri Lesesne, teachers of children's and young adult literature at Sam Houston State University, Huntsville, Texas, and by Adrienne Betz.

About the Author

KAREN HESSE chooses to write for young readers, saying, "I can't think of anyone I'd rather write for." However, she never backs off from difficult issues. She continually offers readers unforgettable heroines who, against a backdrop of adversity, overcome difficulties to emerge stronger, more sure of themselves, more willing to face whatever comes their way. As in *Letters from Rifka*, *The Music of Dolphins*, *Phoenix Rising*, and *A Time of Angels*, Hesse is never afraid to ask the what-if questions, to push her characters to the edge, and to explore the pain of life as well as its joys. Hesse's use of metaphoric language, her development of characters, and her willingness to explore text structure all help make her a cornerstone of the literary world for young readers.

Karen Hesse says, "While growing up in Baltimore,

Maryland, I dreamed of becoming many things: an archaeologist, an ambassador, an actor, an author. In 1969, I attended Towson State College as a theater major but transferred after two semesters to the University of Maryland, where I eventually earned a B.A. in English with double minors in psychology and anthropology.

"From the time I was ten I thought of myself as 'good with words,' thanks to a perceptive and supportive fifth-grade teacher. Mrs. Datnoff believed I could be a professional writer someday, and because she believed, I believed, too. Though I gave up all my other career dreams, I never gave up dreaming of publication. It took more than thirty years to see that fifth-grade dream come true. I don't know whether that makes me extremely patient or just plain stubborn.

"I have earned wages as a waitress, a nanny, a librarian, a personnel officer, an agricultural laborer, an advertising secretary, a typesetter, a proofreader, a mental health care provider, a substitute teacher, and a book reviewer. In and around the edges of all those jobs I have written poems, stories, and books, books, books. The seed for *Out of the Dust* grew out of a picture book idea. Presented with an early draft of my picture book, *Come On, Rain* (Scholastic Press), my writing group insisted I elaborate on why my characters wanted rain so badly. I began researching times when people desperately wanted rain, and *Out of the Dust* blossomed into existence.

"I love writing. I can't wait to get to my keyboard every

morning. I also love reading, hiking, spending time with friends and family, traveling, and music — both playing it and listening to it. National Public Radio is a frequent companion . . . the inspiration for *The Music of Dolphins* came from an interview I heard on *Fresh Air*.

"Young readers are the most challenging, demanding, and rewarding of audiences. Adults often ask why I write for the younger set. My reply: I can't think of anyone I'd rather write for."

Karen Hesse lives in Vermont with her husband and two teenage daughters.

An Interview with Karen Hesse about Out of the Dust

Q. Is there any discovery or experience you particularly hope readers will take away from Out of the Dust?

A. I have determined from the letters I receive from young readers that many of them believe they could never endure the hardships that so many of my fictional characters endure. I portray Billie Jo as an ordinary girl, a girl readers can relate to, who is thrust into extraordinary circumstances from which her first instincts are to turn tail and run. Readers watch Billie Jo struggle with her problems and reach an honest, empowering resolution. If readers come away believing in the ability of Billie Jo to confront, survive, and rise above her life challenges, perhaps they will also glimpse within themselves the strength of character to confront, survive, and rise above the life challenges facing them.

Q. The story is tragic; did you ever consider making it less realistic?

A. I never consider telling any less than the truth in the books I write. It is irresponsible and disrespectful to my readers to sugarcoat life, to leave out the pain. Most readers understand tragedy, most readers understand loss. Even the youngest child understands separation from a loved one, knows the pain of being left behind. Young readers are bright and perceptive, and they can spot a dishonest depiction or a half-truth a mile away. I wouldn't insult them or waste their time with a less than honest portrayal of a time and place and people. True, there is tragedy in *Out of the Dust*, but there is also humor and life, tenderness, decency, kindness, and humanity.

Q. Why blank verse?

A. Sometimes a story can be told with more than the words themselves. Sometimes the form those words take on the page also helps convey the story to the reader. Billie Jo led a spare, bare-boned life. I wanted to convey that life to readers in the form the book took as well as the content. Billie Jo tells her story from a heart that doesn't waste a single beat, from a mouth that doesn't waste a single word. Her trying life demands too much of her physically and emotionally to allow for such waste. Poetry seemed the best way to convey who Billie Jo was and what she had to say.

Q. I assume young people have written to you about the book. What appeals to young readers about the story?

A. One reader confided in me that he, like Billie Jo, had difficulty talking with his father. Another reader had the courage to share the fact that reading did not come easy to him. Because of the poetry format of *Out of the Dust*, he did not feel intimidated by the amount of print on the page and slipped into the book with ease. He felt the freedom to read as little as one or two poems at a sitting. He felt he could move around in the book without getting lost. Consequently he, like many readers I'm hearing from, read this book through without the usual anxiety. Readers tell me that *Out of the Dust* is the first book they've read all the way through in years. Others tell me it is the first they have ever read all the way through. They identify with Billie Jo's struggles, with her sense of isolation and alienation from family, friends, environment.

Q. Why do you choose to write for young people?

A. It is a challenge to create books that will grab young readers and keep them in the story until the end. Young readers lead such busy, complicated lives, they need a book that speaks to them, honestly, respectfully. They deserve the best in their reading experiences. I love a challenge, and creating books readers will take to their hearts is a most compelling and honorable challenge. I read as a way to discover the world and myself through the actions and reactions of fictional others. I write for young readers with the hope that my words may help them in their own explorations of their interior and exterior worlds.

Q. Which books were special to you as a child? Any favorite fictional characters?

A. There are two books I remember had a particular impact on me. One was *Horton Hatches the Egg*. I learned from that book so many things. Here was the abandonment of an egg by its mother, and the extraordinary honor, dedication, and loyalty of the elephant who took over the care of that egg. The second book of great influence on my life was *Hiroshima* by John Hersey. From that account of the bombing of Hiroshima, Japan, I discovered how much grace, integrity, and dignity could be displayed by people under the most extreme circumstances.

Q. *What has winning the Newbery Medal meant to you?*

A. I grew up reading Newbery Award-winning books. I knew when I found that gold seal on a cover I could dive into the pages of the book and feel confident I had entered a world beautifully crafted and rich with substance. I knew I was about to embark on a journey I would never forget, a journey that would change the way I felt about things, would add to my knowledge of the world and myself. To find my own work graced with that gold seal has brought more joy to my heart than I can ever express.

Extracts from Karen Hesse's Newbery Medal Acceptance Speech

Delivered at the Newbery-Caldecott-Wilder Awards Banquet at the American Library Association Annual Convention in Washington, D.C., Sunday, June 28, 1998

I was told once that writing historical fiction was a bad idea. No market for it. I didn't listen. I love research, love dipping into another time and place, and asking the tough questions in a way that helps me see both question and answer with a clearer perspective. *Out of the Dust* is my third historical novel. In the first two, Rifka Nebrot and Hannah Gold brought me back to my Jewish roots. But Billie Jo Kelby brought me even deeper. She brought me back to my human roots.

I can't think about roots of any sort without thinking of my husband, Randy. We have had nearly thirty years together, to listen to each other, to learn from each other. Among his many gifts, Randy has a marvelously green thumb. I, unfortunately, do not.

Once, accidentally, I watered one of Randy's favorite houseplants with vinegar. The plant looked thirsty. I thought I was doing my husband a favor. I didn't know the bottle held vinegar until I had soaked the soil, until the sharp acid filtered down through the rich dirt toward the roots. The plant died.

It couldn't have done otherwise.

The innocent substitution of one liquid for another . . . it happens. In *Out of the Dust*, when Billie Jo's mother reaches for the pail, she thinks she, too, is reaching for water, pouring water to make coffee. She doesn't realize her mistake, that she is pouring kerosene, until the flames rise up from the stove.

Readers ask, could such a terrible mistake really happen? Yes. It happened often. I based the accident on a series of articles appearing in the 1934 *Boise City News*. That particular family tragedy planted the seed for *Out of the Dust*, as much as the dust storms did.

Let me tell you. I never make up any of the bad things that happen to my characters. I love my characters too much to hurt them deliberately, even the prickly ones. It just so happens that in life, there's pain; sorrow lives in the shadow of joy, joy in the shadow of sorrow. The question is, do we let the pain reign triumphant, or do we find a way to grow, to transform, and ultimately transcend our pain?

The first traceable roots for *Out of the Dust* reach back to 1993 when I took a car trip out to Colorado with fellow author Liza Ketchum. When we entered Kansas something extraordinary happened. I fell in love. I had never been in the interior of the country before. Our first day in Kansas we experienced a tornado. I watched, awestruck as the sky turned green as a bruise and the air swelled with explosive energy. The second day in Kansas, we walked in a town so small it didn't have a name. It grew up beside a railroad track and never fully pulled itself from the earth. The wind never stopped blowing there. It caressed our faces, it whispered in our ears. The grass moved like a corps of dancers. The colors were unlike any I had ever encountered on the East Coast or the West. And the sky and land went on to the horizon and beyond.

It took me three years to internalize that experience enough to write about it. I had been working on a picture book in which a young inner-city child longs for rain. My writing group loved the language but had problems with the main character's motivation. The question, as it usually does, came from Eileen Christelow. She asked, "Where's the emotional line here? Why does this child want it to rain so much?" I later captured the motivation, the emotional line of that picture book, even to Eileen's satisfaction, but at that moment, instead, my mind slid precipitously back sixty years to a time when people desperately wanted rain, to the dirty thirties.

But how could I recreate the dust bowl? I was born in 1952, in Baltimore, Maryland. What did I know from dust? I knew alley dust, I knew gutter dust, but what did I know of dust so extensive it blew from one state to another, across an entire nation, and out over the ocean where it rained down on the decks of ships hundreds of miles out to sea?

I phoned the Oklahoma Historical Society and asked for help. I'd found, in one of the very dry treatises on Plains agricultural practices, a reference to the *Boise City News*, a daily paper published in the Oklahoma Panhandle during the period in which I was most interested. The Oklahoma Historical Society allowed as how there had been such a paper. I asked if I might get copies of it. Yes, they said, it was available on microfilm. So off went my check to purchase the film, and when the package arrived, with giddy excitement, I rushed to my local library, and took possession of the microfilm machine, proclaiming it my exclusive property for weeks, while I dug in and lived through day after day, month after month, year after year of life in the heart of the Depression, in the heart of the dust bowl. I saturated myself with those dusty, dirty, desperate times, and what I discovered thrilled me. I had thought it never rained during that period. In fact it did. Only rarely did the rain do any good. But it did rain. And through that grim time, when men jumped to their deaths from tall buildings and farmers shot themselves behind barns, I discovered there was still life going on, talent shows, dances, movies. Daily acts of generosity and kindness. Living through those dirty years, article by article, in the pages of the *Boise City News*, supplied the balance of what I needed to recreate credibly that extraordinary time and place.

I gave the manuscript to my daughters first. A novel in free verse, I didn't know if anyone would understand what I was trying to do. But both Kate and Rachel handed the limp pages back, hours later, their eyes welled with tears. Okay, I thought. They must have understood a little bit. I revised the manuscript based on Kate's and Rachel's comments, and gave it next to Liza and Eileen. They asked a lot of questions, but for once they didn't ask about emotional line. I revised the manuscript again, according to Liza's and Eileen's comments.

The next time I sent it to my editor. "It'll be great," she said. "But I want you to think, what is it about, really? What is going on with Billie Jo and Pa, what is going on with Billie Jo and Ma? And what is going on with Billie Jo herself?"

And I knew. It was about forgiveness. The whole book. Every relationship. Not only the relationships between people, but the relationship between the people and the land itself. It was all about forgiveness.

I began my literary life as a poet. When I was expecting my first child, my ability to focus on the creation of poetry diminished as my need to focus on the creation of human life increased. For seventeen years my brain continued to place the nurturing of my daughters above all other creative endeavors and I forsook poetry. Not that prose is easy to write. But for me, at least, it required a different commitment of brain cells, a different commitment of energy and emotion. Part of my mind always listened for my children during those years. And that listening rendered me incapable of writing poetry. But something inexplicably wonderful happened. My daughters grew up. They reached an age of independence and self-possession that for the first time in seventeen years permitted my brain to let go of them for minutes, hours at a time, and in those minutes and hours, poetry was allowed to return and *Out of the Dust* to be born. I never attempted to write this book any other way than in free verse. The frugality of the life, the hypnotically hard work of farming, the grimness of conditions during the dust bowl, demanded an economy of words. Pa and Ma and Billie Jo's rawboned life translated into poetry, and bless Scholastic for honoring that translation and producing *Out of the Dust* with the spare understatement I sought when writing it.

I have so much respect for these people, these survivors of the dust, the Arley and Vera Wanderdales, the Mad Dog Craddocks, the Joe De La Flors. I discovered Joe in WPA material on the Internet and wove him in, a Mexican-American cowboy, hardworking, unacknowledged. I put him up high in the saddle where he belonged, where Billie Jo could look up to him.

Occasionally, adult readers grimace at the events documented in *Out of the Dust*. They ask, how can this book be for young readers? I ask, how can it not? The children I have met during my travels around the country have astounded me, with their perception, their intelligence, their capacity to take in information and apply it to a greater picture, or take in the greater picture and distill it down to what they need from it.

Young readers are asking for substance. They are asking for respect. They are asking for books that challenge, and confirm, and console. They are asking for us to listen to their questions and to help them find their own answers. If we cannot attend always to those questions, to that quest for answers, whether our work is that of librarian, writer, teacher, publisher, or parent, how can they forgive us? And yet they do, every day. Just as Billie Jo forgave Ma. Just as Billie Jo forgave Pa. Just as Billie Jo forgave herself. And with that forgiveness Billie Jo finally set her roots and turned toward her future.

Often, our lives are so crowded, we need to weed out what is essential, what is not. Reading historical fiction gives us perspective. It gives us respite from the tempest of our present-day lives. It gives us a safe place in which we can grow, transform, transcend. It helps us understand, that sometimes the questions are too hard, that sometimes there are no answers, that sometimes there is only forgiveness.

Hodding Carter said, "There are only two lasting bequests we can hope to give our children. One of these is roots, the other wings." Ellen Fader, members of the Newbery committee, members of the ALA, from the girl who devoured Newberys in a corner of the Enoch Pratt Free Library, thank you.

Critical Acclaim for Out of the Dust

★ "**A powerfully compelling tale** of a girl with enormous strength, courage, and love.... An excellent book for discussion, and many of the poems stand alone sufficiently to be used as powerful supplements to a history lesson."
— *Booklist*, starred review

★ "**Wonderful . . . Hesse's ever-growing skill** as a writer willing to take chances with her form shines through superbly."
— *School Library Journal*, starred review

★ "**Readers may find their own feelings** swaying in beat with the heroine's shifting moods."
— *Publishers Weekly*, starred review

"**A glimpse of beauty** wrought from brutal reality."
— *Kirkus Reviews*

"**A thoughtful and provocative book** for classrooms and libraries." — *Voice of Youth Advocates*, 5Q 4P

"**[Billie Jo's] voice**, nearly every word informed by longing, provides an immediacy that expressively depicts both a grim historical era and one family's healing." — *Horn Book*

Awards and Honors for Out of the Dust

1998 Newbery Medal

1998 Scott O'Dell Award for Historical Fiction

ALA Notable Children's Book

ALA Best Book for Young Adults

School Library Journal Best Book of the Year

Booklist Editors' Choice

Book Links "Lasting Connection"

Publishers Weekly Best Book of the Year

New York Public Library Children's Book of the

Year—100 Titles for Reading and Sharing

To order copies of Out of the Dust (Hardcover, 0-590-36080-9, $15.95; Paperback, 0-590-37125-8, $4.99), contact your local bookstore or usual supplier, or call toll-free: 1-800-SCHOLASTIC.

Other Books by Karen Hesse
Available from Scholastic

The Music of Dolphins

Rescued after living with dolphins as a wild child, sixteen-year-old Mila learns human language and faces a choice between two different worlds.

An ALA Best Book for Young Adults
A *School Library Journal* Best Book of the Year
A *Book Links* Best Book of the Year
A *Publishers Weekly* Best Book of the Year

★ "This powerful exploration of how we become human and how the soul endures is a song of beauty and sorrow, haunting and unforgettable."
—*School Library Journal*, starred review

★ "As moving as a sonnet, as eloquently structured as a bell curve, this book poignantly explores the most profound themes—what it means to be human. . . . All together, a frequently dazzling novel." —*Publishers Weekly*, starred review

Ages 11 up
Hardcover: 0-590-89797-7, $14.95
Paperback: 0-590-89798-5, $4.50

Just Juice
with pictures by Robert Andrew Parker

Third-grader Juice Faulstich lives with her family in the North Carolina hills. She can't seem to learn to read — but she has other talents that help pull her family through some hard times.

Ages 8 up
Hardcover: 0-590-03382-4, $14.95

Come On, Rain
illustrated by Jon J. Muth

Exquisite language and acute observation depict the glorious experience of a refreshing and long-awaited summer rain.

Ages 4 up
Hardcover: 0-590-33125-6, $15.95

OTHER BOOKS BY KAREN HESSE
Wish on a Unicorn (1991), Henry Holt
Letters from Rifka (1992), Henry Holt
Poppy's Chair (1993), Macmillan
Lester's Dog (1993), Crown
Lavender (1993), Holt
Sable (1994), Holt
Phoenix Rising (1994), Holt
A Time of Angels (1995), Hyperion

Prices and availability are subject to change without notice.